———————————— ★ ————————————

"Something peculiar happe⸺

"What?" Rena was tiring. She leaned heavily on her elbows.

"I saw a customer give Old Sam a wad of folding money for a thirty-five-cent paperback. Really strange."

Rena had stiffened as I spoke. She looked at me with shuttered eyes. "So?"

"So…well…" I stumbled, taken aback at the hostility in her voice. "I just thought you might know what that was all about."

"No," she said stonily. "I do not." Her gaze slid away from my face.

"Well…" I stood up, mystified. She was obviously lying and doing it badly.

———————————— ★ ————————————

# NEXT WEEK WILL BE —WILL BE— BETTER

# JEAN RURYK

**WORLDWIDE.®**

TORONTO • NEW YORK • LONDON
AMSTERDAM • PARIS • SYDNEY • HAMBURG
STOCKHOLM • ATHENS • TOKYO • MILAN
MADRID • WARSAW • BUDAPEST • AUCKLAND

**NEXT WEEK WILL BE BETTER**

A Worldwide Mystery/December 1999

First published by St. Martin's Press, Incorporated.

ISBN 0-373-26333-3

Visit us at www.worldwidemystery.com

**Printed in U.S.A.**

For Sasha

# ONE

I HAD BEEN filling in for Rena at flea markets for two weeks when Old Sam was murdered.

Rena had dropped by in mid June on her way home from working Finney's Farm, a flea market held every Friday about forty-five miles from town.

If your day begins at four in the morning, as Rena's had, you're in no mood for casual socializing at five-thirty in the afternoon. So when her van swung into my driveway I straightened up from snipping deadheads from the marigolds and watched it approach, more than mildly curious.

The van rolled to a halt a few feet away from me. Rena switched off the engine and leaned out the driver's window.

"Hallo, Cat'rine." Weariness intensified her normally slight accent.

"I took the chance you would be home."

"Hi, Rena. Good to see you. What's wrong?"

"Something has to be wrong?" She picked up a brown paper bag from the bucket seat beside her. "The Art Deco drawer pulls you asked me to keep an eye out for? I found some today," she said, taking one out of the bag and handing it to me. "Eight of them. If you like, good. If not I can sell them."

The pull was a beauty. Brass, molded in the shape of a quarter melon, with a stylized red enamel tulip centered between the spikes of two green enamel leaves.

"It's perfect." I turned the pull over in my hand. "Of course I'll take them. But you didn't have to come all this way. I'd have picked them up."

Rena shrugged.

"It was either I deliver or you wait a long time. I go into hospital Sunday."

"Hospital? What's wrong?"

"Gallstones. Not so serious."

"Not much fun, either." I handed the drawer pull back. "Why don't you come in? I'll pay you for these and make us a cup of tea."

Rena opened the car door and stepped down from the van. She pressed her fists into the small of her back and stretched, grimacing.

If I didn't know Rena is in her early fifties I'd guess her to be my age, or older. She is the only woman I know who seems to be completely without vanity.

She's overweight, carrying at least forty extra pounds on a small frame. Her hair is gray and she cuts it herself, chopping haphazardly when her bangs grow long enough to threaten her vision. Her eyes are gray, pale and deep-set in a face darkened to a dry and coppery brown by years of exposure to sun, wind, and weather. I doubt she ever uses skin cream and I'll bet my house she doesn't even own a lipstick.

I've known her for at least nine years and I've never seen her dressed in anything but oversize T-shirts, brown polyester knit pants, and white Reeboks.

She booted the car door shut with her heel.

"I don't know about tea," she said. "But maybe I could use your bathroom? There was the usual lineup at Finney's."

"They still have only one washroom?"

"They put in some Porta Potties here and there, up in the parking lot." Rena followed me into the house. "Too far for the vendors. The men still wee-wee behind the barn."

"Behind the barn where the grass don't grow. I remember that." I pointed down the hall. "The bathroom's thataway."

"Thank you." She handed me the paper bag. "The pulls."

Rena turned left, I went right, to the kitchen, where I plugged in the kettle, spooned Earl Grey into the teapot, and opened the bag of drawer pulls.

I'm not particularly fond of the Art Deco period. Some of my dislike probably stems from the fact that I was a child in the Depression years. The veneered waterfall furniture and the coldly linear designs are reminders of the bleakness and despair of that era. I'm sixty-two now, and those days are long gone. But, like most members of my generation, much of what I am now was shaped by the Dirty Thirties. None of us survived untouched.

Still, I could appreciate the craftsmanship that had gone into the fashioning of the drawer pulls. They were handmade, hand-painted, and exactly right for the vanity I was in the process of restoring.

"Catherine?" Rena appeared in the doorway. "I used one of the washcloths off the shelf. Is that all right?"

"That's what they're there for." I held up one of the pulls. "What do I owe you?"

"Sixteen. I paid two dollars each for them."

"I'll pay twenty-five." I reached for my cash jar. "You have to make something on them."

"We have had this argument before. One does not make money from one's friends. End of story." Rena tilted her head and sniffed appreciatively. "Something smells good."

"Baked macaroni."

I withdrew a ten, a five, and four quarters from the jar and handed the money to her. She stuffed it into the black canvas kangaroo pouch on her belt and thanked me.

"Why not have dinner with me?" I said. "I always make too much of everything and it's ready now. You can eat and run. You won't have to cook when you get home."

She hesitated. Then she sighed, fatigue making the decision for her.

"Thank you," she said. "But let me help. Where is it you keep your dishes?"

"In the cupboard above the dishwasher. Cutlery is in the drawer to the left."

I crossed to the fridge to get the Caesar salad I had prepared earlier, then slipped oven mitts on, removed the macaroni from the oven and carried it to the table.

We ate in silence for a minute or two, Rena frowning and preoccupied. As much to make conversation as anything I asked her how long she expected to be out of commission.

"The doctor said it would be at least six weeks before I should lift and carry." Her frown deepened. "Too long. I will lose my space at Finney's."

"How do you mean, lose your space? I thought Finney's was on a first-come basis."

"No more in the paved section. It is all now reserved. When I am no-show for three weeks I will lose my spot."

"What are they going to do? Toss you out in the cow pasture?"

"Yes."

I had spoken flippantly, unthinking. Rena's three-letter answer hit the table with a dull thud. I glanced up at her. She was poking aimlessly at her salad.

"But you've been setting up at Finney's for the last ten years," I protested. "They know you."

"So they know me." Rena made a sour face. "Such a big deal. There are so many vendors wishing for space they don't know anybody. It is different now, Catherine. Vendors park in the field the night before. They sleep in their vans so they have a spot in the morning.''

"What about Beacon Mall? Three strikes and you're out there too?''

Rena nodded glumly.

She had good reason to be despondent.

Finney's is an outdoor summer flea market, open from early May to late October. The peak selling months are July and August, when tourists, cottagers from the nearby lake district, and holiday people with nothing better to do descend en masse.

After deducting operating expenses—gas and rental, plus whatever she had paid for her merchandise—Rena could count on clearing at least three thousand dollars for the twenty-week period. Setting up in the field might possibly affect her take. And it might not. But it would certainly make an already long and arduous day even more difficult.

Beacon Mall, a year-round indoor flea market, presented the real problem. All spaces were reserved. And there was no cow pasture to take up the slack. Losing Beacon would mean Rena would have no outlet through the winter months. She'd be wiped out.

I studied her as she stolidly chewed her salad. A fragment of romaine lettuce clung to her lower lip. I tried to imagine a job she would qualify for and couldn't visualize her as anything but a flea market vendor. Or a charwoman.

Unworthy thought. There had to be a way out for her.

"Couldn't you let some other vendor occupy your spaces for the weeks you're away?" I suggested. "Give them back to you when you're ready?"

Rena almost smiled. "They wouldn't give them back," she said. "And it is not permitted to transfer reservations."

Oh, hell. There really was only one way. I drew a deep breath and pushed my plate aside.

"Okay." I said. "Suppose I were to fill in for you at Finney's and Beacon? You could tell them I'm your sister. Or your old maiden aunt, whatever. Would that hold your spaces until you're able to take over again?"

A gleam of hope flickered briefly in Rena's pale eyes. It faded and she shook her head.

"I appreciate very much the offer, Catherine," she said. "But I think you forget how much labor it is."

"I remember exactly. Believe me, I have no desire to make a career of it. But a few weeks won't kill me."

"Perhaps it would be six weeks. Too much."

"Six weeks is only twelve days of setting up," I said. "Face it, Rena. Even if you go back to Finney's when you're well enough, sleeping in a van is no pajama party. And you can't afford to lose Beacon at all.''

Rena studied my face. Her gaze slid away, roamed the wall behind me. She frowned, the grooves between her heavy, unplucked brows deepening. Then she sighed.

''All right,'' she said. ''But I make two conditions. One, if it becomes too much, you must stop. And you must take twenty-five percent of what you sell.''

''Yes on one. Two, no. I won't take your profit.''

''Ten percent.''

''One does not make money from one's friends. End of story.'' I gathered the empty plates, carried them to the sink, and reached into the cupboard for cups. ''When do you go into the hospital?''

''Sunday night. After Beacon.''

''Want me to drive you down?''

Rena shook her head. ''Thank you, Catherine. My tenant upstairs, Frank Czerny, will take me in.''

I brought the teapot to the table, sat down, and poured for each of us. Rena sipped, frowning thoughtfully.

''My tables are too long for your car,'' she said. ''You must take my van.''

''That's fine. When can I pick it up?''

''Would Monday be good? I will arrange to leave the keys with Frank, upstairs.''

''Monday would be fine,'' I agreed. ''Are you

still pricing the way you used to? Allowing a ten-percent haggling margin?''

"More or less." Rena set her teacup down heavily. "I am sorry, Catherine. I am very tired. Would it offend you if I leave without finishing?''

I pushed my chair back. "Of course not.''

As I walked her out to her van, I asked Rena which hospital she was entering.

"I'll come and visit," I offered.

"Please, no." She opened the van door and turned to face me. "I am a most unpleasant patient. Let me call you.''

She climbed into the van and closed the door, frowning down at me through the open window.

"You are certain you wish to do this, Catherine?'' she said dubiously. "It is eight years since you were in the flea markets. Things have changed.''

"Don't worry. I'll be fine. Go.''

I waved her off, thinking what's to change? You set up, you sell, you pack up and go home.

Simple.

# TWO

MIKE MELNYK swung his peg leg into the car and slid into the passenger seat beside me.

"I haven't had any breakfast," he grumbled. "Can we stop for coffee somewhere?"

"Can you survive without it?"

"Do I have to?"

"I'd like to get this over with. I'll make brunch for you when we get back."

"Pancakes?"

"Sure."

"Then I guess I'll survive."

Mike's an ex-newspaperman, a former crime reporter and columnist. I couldn't drive two cars back from Rena's and I had called him, asking for help. He had bitched volubly, but he had come.

He's an opinionated and irascible man. He's also sharp, funny, and a very good friend.

Twenty-odd years ago he lost his wife and his left leg to a car bomb intended for another man. He never went back to the paper. He began compiling a book on organized crime, a book I have a sneaking suspicion he'll never complete. I don't think he wants to see it finished.

He adjusted his prosthesis, settled his rump into

the bucket seat, yanked the seat belt across his barrel chest, and fastened it, grunting like a bear who has arranged his snoozing territory to perfection.

"So," he said. "Who is this bimbo we're going to all the effort for?"

"She's not a bimbo. Her name's Irena." I pronounced it the way Rena did, Ee-ray-nah. "Kundera. Rena. I met her back when I was selling off all the junk in my house at flea markets."

"Kundera? There's a writer named Kundera. Milan Kundera. Czechoslovakian, I think. Any relation?"

"I don't know. Rena's Czech. She never mentioned a writer relative, but I suppose it's possible."

I shifted into reverse and twisted in my seat, neck craned to see out the rear window. Backing up a car isn't one of the things I do well.

Safely down the driveway and out into the street, I continued, "Rena and her husband emigrated when Soviet troops invaded Czechoslovakia in 'sixty-eight."

"Uh." Mike withdrew a cigarette from the pack in his shirt pocket and began his ritual search for matches, a habit that irks me out of all proportion.

"Oh for Christ's sake, Mike. Stop flailing about. Use the damn lighter."

He leaned forward and punched it in, grinning sideways at me.

"Cranky, are we? What's the matter, Cat? Worried you've bitten off more than you can chew?"

"Don't be ridiculous. I've done flea markets before. I know what's involved. I'm not worried."

"No?" Mike withdrew the lighter, applied it to his cigarette, and returned it to the dash. He blew out a luxurious stream of smoke and settled back smugly. "Okay, you're not worried. So, inform me. Exactly what is involved?"

"It's no big deal. On Friday I set up at Finney's Farm. On Sunday I set up at Beacon Mall."

"That's it?"

"That's it," I said as I accelerated up the ramp to the crosstown expressway.

Mike waited until we had blended into the stream of traffic, then said, "Maybe I'll go with you to this Finney place on Friday. I've never been to a flea market. You want company?"

"I'd love it." I gave him a broad, sweet smile. "I'll pick you up at four-thirty Friday morning."

"Four-thirty!" His head reared back. "In the *morning?* What the hell for?"

"Because by the time we get there, unload, and set up it'll be six o'clock."

"So? Who the hell goes to a flea market at six in the morning?"

"Antique dealers. Pickers. Collectors. Most of them are there before sunrise, scooting around with their flashlights before the vendors are even set up."

"You're kidding. Why, for God's sake?"

"That's when the good stuff goes."

"Good stuff? What kind of good stuff are we talking about here?"

"For the antique dealers and pickers? Anything they can make a buck on. For the collectors, one more."

Mike leaned forward and mashed his cigarette butt in the ashtray. "One more what?" he asked.

I slid the ashtray back under the dashboard. Since I quit smoking the acrid smell of dead tobacco has become particularly offensive.

"One more anything. You name it, somebody collects it. And flea markets are a good place to find it."

"At four in the morning?"

"Four in the morning is mainly dealers looking for a find."

Mike shook his head. "Crazy. So you'll be getting up before dawn twice a week?"

"Once. I won't get up until five-thirty on Sundays. Beacon doesn't open till seven."

"Same difference," Mike grunted. "This Rena must be one hell of a good friend. How come you've never mentioned her?"

"I haven't? I must have."

"Never," Mike said positively. "You have never mentioned Ee-ray-nah Kundera. I'd have remembered the name."

I threw a disconcerted glance at him.

Behind his frowning brown eyes, under that balding pate, there's a newspaper morgue of a mind, randomly packed with names, dates, and events, filed and never forgotten. If he claimed I had never spoken of Rena, I knew it had to be so.

For some reason, I found the thought disturbing.

I'd first met Rena at Finney's Farm, the morning I set up to sell off the lesser collectibles and junk from the house I had purchased. She was watching me trying to cope with the feeding frenzy of dealers, two-deep around my table as I unpacked.

Hands were grabbing articles before I could set them down. Total strangers were scrabbling in my boxes, tearing at the newspaper wrappings. Nothing had been priced and a cacophony of voices demanded how much, hey, what're you asking for this? what's your dealer's discount? how much?

As I was beginning to panic, she was suddenly beside me, fending off the dealers, calling most of them by name.

"Please. Give her a chance. One at a time." She swung on me, a McCoy planter in her hands. "How much?"

I told her. For the next twenty minutes, she dickered with the dealers and took their money. I made change, wrapped and bagged the articles, working as fast as I could.

Then, as suddenly as it had begun, the rush ended. We were alone. The dealers had flown, migrating like a flock of noisome crows, to converge on a vendor down the aisle who had just opened his van doors.

"My God," I panted. "Is it always like this?"

She shook her head. "You are a new face. They have hope for new stuff."

She gestured to the tables set up in the space next to mine, where a woman in a bright red straw hat bent to examine a large tureen.

"I am there," she explained. "You excuse me, I have a customer. My name is Rena. If you have need of help, ask."

"I'm Catherine," I called to her retreating back, "and thank you."

She didn't look back. "No problem," she said.

The following week, we found ourselves side by side once more. On the third Friday, we changed our setup from two individual U's to an L and a reverse L, with our vehicles at the rear and ourselves in the middle. Whichever of us arrived first saved the space next door for the other.

The new arrangement permitted us greater freedom to go for a walk and shop if we chose, to go to the washroom if we had to, and to chat during the lulls.

We talked about our husbands.

Mine, whom I had left after finally admitting to myself that his sole aim in life was to drink every distillery in the country dry. Hers, whose cancer had metastasized with devastating speed and killed him within six short and agonizing weeks.

We talked of our children.

My daughter Laurie, who was twenty then, and

in college. Her son Stepan, thirteen years old, born when she was thirty-six, a Down's syndrome child.

She told me she and her husband had worked together, cleaning banks at night and slowly acquiring a client list, building a business of their own, their American dream. My former career as a producer of television commercials had intrigued her.

Her dream collapsed when her husband died. My career melted away when a drunk driver smashed into the location van in which I was a passenger. By the time I was able to work again, the world had moved on.

Mortgage insurance had enabled Rena to keep the duplex she and Jan had scrimped for, but her only source of income was rent from the upper apartment. Searching for a way to make money, a way that would allow her to keep Stepan, then three years old, with her, she discovered flea markets.

"I made a start the hard way. I did home baking. Pies, muffins, cookies," Rena reminisced. "Then I saw what the others sold and I also ran to the garage sales and to estate sales and auctions. When I had enough stock I let drop the baking." With a rare flash of humor, she added, "I have not turned on the oven since."

When October came and the outdoor flea markets closed down, we set up together at Beacon Mall for the winter. The following spring we were back at Finney's.

At summer's end, with all the junk disposed of, I quit flea marketing.

We never socialized. Not then, not since. Months go by during which we don't see one another. Yet when my daughter Laurie and her husband Andy were killed in a freak car accident, I phoned Rena. And when Stepan had to be placed in an institution—he had been arrested for touching a child on the street—she called me.

"But other than our flea-marketing year together we don't really have much in common," I summed up to Mike. He had listened to me talk without comment. "I've been able to steer her to some profitable estate sales through Charlie and Rafe. She'll dig through the flea markets for me when I need the odd thing. We're useful to one another. Does that make us more than friends or less than friends?"

"More, less. What difference? You take from one another. That's what friendship is."

I shot him a startled glance. "That's pretty cynical, isn't it?"

"What's so cynical about it? It's true."

Mike withdrew a cigarette from his shirt pocket. His hand moved toward his jacket pocket, faltered, and changed direction. He punched the dash lighter into its socket.

"Cat, you don't become friends—and you don't remain friends—with people who haven't anything to give you."

"You really believe that?"

"Damn right, I do. Otherwise, you'd be ass deep in friends. None of whom would be doing you one damn bit of good." He pulled out the lighter and lit his cigarette.

"Come off it, Mike. We don't choose our friends for what we can get from them."

"Sure we do. Maybe we choose to be friends with people simply because they make us laugh. Or people who make us feel good about ourselves. Or because they're interesting or smart and we can learn something from them. Or for moral support. Or even because they treat us like shit and feed the martyr complex we didn't know we had. Whatever. The truth is, we don't become friends with people who don't have anything to give us."

"I don't know," I said doubtfully. "I don't think I've ever chosen friends because they might be useful."

"Sure you have. We all do. That's what friendship is about. The giving and taking between two people of what each needs from the other. When there's nothing more to give or take, the friendship dies. *'The friends I've made have slipped and strayed and who's the one to care...'* Who wrote that?"

"Dorothy Parker. *'A loathsome lot and best forgot.'*"

"There you go."

"Uh."

My exit loomed ahead and I concentrated on

moving to the outside lane. I took the long, slow, downramp curve, mulling over the nature of my friendship with Rena.

"You know, Mike," I said when we reached street level, "there's a sort of bond that forms between the regular flea market vendors. Even with vendors you don't like much. I detested Shifty George and Miss Piggy, but if—"

"Shifty George? Miss Piggy? You're kidding."

"No, I'm not. Shifty George is a nasty little Hungarian. He's called Shifty because that's what he is. Also, to differentiate him from Saint George, who's a born-again Bible-thumping bore."

"And Miss Piggy? I take it that's who she looks like?"

"Right. A particularly repulsive Miss Pig."

"They're called these names to their faces?"

"Of course not! That's just what we call them when we talk about them."

"I see," Mike said smugly. "Tell me more about this wonderful bond between vendors."

The traffic light ahead turned yellow. I stepped on the brake and looked across at Mike. He was grinning that dumb clown grin of his.

"God, I hate it when you go wise-ass," I said.

"Hey, Cat. You walked right into it. So. Tell me about this bonding thing."

"Oh, hell. I guess it's not a bonding thing. It's a *'we'* and *'them'* thing. We, the vendors. Them, everybody else."

The light changed to green. I accelerated through the intersection.

"There used to be two vendors who set up together," I said when we were beyond the traffic lights. "They were gay. And it so happened they were both named Peter. We called them Pete One and Pete Two, until someone pointed out that *pitou* is a French word for a small dog. It was perfect. Pete Two was a nasty little terrier, skinny and yappy and vicious. So he became Pitou. Pete and Pitou."

"You're making this up," Mike said.

"No. I'm not."

I turned right on Oliver, an avenue of duplexes, row on row, one of which was Rena's.

"Pete was big and fat and pouty and every bit as mean as Pitou. He was also very, very flitty. He minced. He twittered a lot. He stuck teeny-weeny pink satin bows on every itty-bitty piece on their table. Rena and I had the booth across from then at Beacon Mall the winter I was there."

I leaned past Mike to check the house numbers. The duplexes were identical, one beside the next, and I was never certain which was Rena's. We were close.

"Anyway," I continued, "I was out in the aisle talking with Old Sam one Sunday when one of the customers walked up to us. He was a regular at Beacon, collected war memorabilia. One of those high-testosterone individuals who wear baseball caps?"

"I know the type."

"He came up to us and made a loud remark about the limp-wristed faggot across the way putting a pink bow on a World War Two brass shell casing, har-dee-har. Old Sam gave him a big wide smile and said, 'Yeah. Ain't it awful. But I'll tell you something, old buddy. I'd rather have his limp wrist than your red neck.' The creep huffed off and left me gaping at Old Sam. 'I thought you detested them, Pete and Pitou,' I said."

There was an empty space at the curb. I sidled into it quickly and switched off the motor.

"'I do,' Old Sam said. 'They're bitches, both of them. But they're *our* bitches.'"

# THREE

FRANK CZERNY was a stocky man in his early thirties, with pale eyes behind steel-rimmed glasses and a friendly smile. He peered past me to where Mike waited at the curb.

"I'm Frank, Mrs. Wilde." He extended his hand, took mine in a firm grip. "We've been waiting for you. Lucie insists I invite you and your husband up for coffee."

"Not husband. Friend," I said as we released my hand. I eyed the staircase rising steeply behind him.

"I'm sorry, Frank. Maybe next time. Mike has a problem with stairs. But would you please thank Lucie?"

Frank nodded. Mounting the stairs two at a time, he disappeared through a door on the landing above. Moments later he reappeared carrying a gray tin box. Behind him, a young woman with a small child squirming in her arms smiled down at me.

"Hello, Mrs. Wilde," she called. "I'm Lucie."

She positioned the little boy, whose hair was as fiery as his mother's, on her left hip and followed her husband down the stairs, talking as she descended.

"Can I call you Catherine? Irena has told me so much about you, I feel as if I know you. Be still, Brandon, or I'll drop you on your head. She wasn't anxious about the operation, you know. All she worried about was losing her spot at the flea market. I'm glad she had you."

She reached ground level and set her son down on the tiled floor. Brandon lurched the three steps it took to wrap his arms around his father's leg.

Frank handed the tin box to me.

"This is Rena's cash float," he said. He lifted the boy and slung him fireman style over his shoulder. "The van is in the garage. We'll drive it out for you."

"Thank you." I started down the walk to where Mike waited, Lucie beside me. "Will you be visiting Rena in the hospital?" I asked.

"No. She doesn't want visitors. We'll pick her up on Sunday and bring her home."

"Do you think she'll be all right, home alone?" I stopped and faced Lucie, frowning. "I didn't think of it before. Maybe you should bring her to my place. For the first week, anyway."

Lucie shook her head. "You know Irena," she said. "Don't worry, I'm right upstairs. If she needs anything all she has to do is bang on the pipes."

She smiled, revealing a narrow gap between her front teeth. She had a redhead's pale, translucent skin, dusted lightly with freckles. Her eyes were amber, her lashes and brows pale gold. It wasn't a pretty face, but her smile was generous and sweet.

"Are you and Rena related?" I smiled back at her.

"No. She's our landlady. And our friend." Lucie crossed her arms over her thin chest and looked back at the duplex, up at the second floor, her home.

"She's our friend," she repeated, her voice low, her eyes on the open garage doors through which Frank had carried their son. "Three years ago, Frank lost his job. He's a baker, you know, and the company went bankrupt. We went three months without a cent coming in. We didn't have any money saved, and I was pregnant. It was terrible."

"I can imagine. You didn't try to get welfare?"

"Frank wouldn't go on welfare. He said once you get on you never get off. My aunt brought us food, we didn't starve, but she has only a small pension." She turned to me, her eyes appealing for understanding. "My Frank is a very proud man."

I nodded. "I can see that."

"You can?" Her face lit up. "Irena did too. The whole three months she didn't ask for her rent money, not once, and when Frank finally got a job she let us pay her back a bit at a time. Frank thinks the world of her, Catherine. He'd do anything for her. Me too. So let us take care of Irena. You take care of her flea markets."

"I will. Don't worry."

Frank brought Rena's van to a halt beside us. He

climbed down, handed Brandon to his wife, and proceeded to instruct me, carefully and methodically,
on the handling of the van. I listened, but he could
have saved himself the effort. My mind went blank
after step two. Spoken directions are lost on me. I
have to either read or do.

I waved good-bye, hoping I would at least be out
of sight before I stalled out or did something equally
inept.

Mike drove my station wagon. I followed. He lost
me long before we reached the expressway and was
waiting when I rolled into my driveway. His face
was a thundercloud.

"Don't say it," I warned, staggering from the
van.

I was thoroughly rattled. The brakes in Rena's
van were soft, the left turn signal had to be turned
off by hand, the rearview mirror reflected nothing
but boxes piled one on top of the other in back, and
I had forgotten to adjust the side mirrors. And I
hadn't driven a manual shift in years.

"Don't tell me what to say, godammit. I was beginning to get worried. A couple more minutes and
I'd have gone back looking for you."

"All right. *All right.* I'm sorry. I've never driven
one of these bloody beasts before." I slammed the
van door. "You didn't have to wait for me. You
could have gone home."

"Yeah, sure. After cooling my ass out here for

over half an hour, wondering what the hell's happened to you? Wouldn't you be worried?''

"About you? Sterling Moss incarnate? Hell no.''

"Thanks a whole bunch," Mike snarled.

"You're welcome. Are you coming in for brunch?''

"No I'm not." He turned and stumped angrily to where his car was parked.

"Mike," I called after him, "thanks for the help."

He ignored me. He opened the car door, hoisted himself into the driver's seat, and slammed the door. The motor sprang to life.

At the foot of the driveway, he honked the horn and flapped a farewell hand out the window, then screeched a left turn into the street.

I took the tin box into the house and set it on the kitchen table. It contained fifty dollars float money in small bills and coins. There was a dark blue card, about three by five inches, with the numbers nine-three-six in reverse white, over which had been rubber-stamped a smudged circle bearing indecipherable lettering. There was also a note from Rena.

*Catherine,*
  *Look for Sam at Finney's. He has space #35. Mine is next to his. He knows you are coming.*
                              *Thank you again,*
                                          *Rena*

# FOUR

FINNEY'S FARM hasn't been a working farm for fifty years or more.

There are various and colorful legends as to who Finney was, the most enduring being that:

a. Finney was a bootlegger who made his fortune in illegal booze, abandoned the farm when prohibition was repealed and returned to the Ould Sod to lend his talents to the IRA, and:

b. Finney had been the farm's wide-roving and horny Irish Setter whose distinctive coloring still shows up, generations later, in farm dogs throughout three counties.

Thirty years ago, the farm was purchased from the county by a livestock auctioneer whose first name was Vladimir and whose surname was unpronounceable. He bought the scrubby outfit to acquire the magnificent barns.

There are two of them, one very large, both constructed from native field stones and cedar planks. Their sheet metal roofs are an electrifying crimson, repainted every year, and are visible for miles in any direction.

The flea market evolved slowly.

In the beginning, Vladimir—forget the Vladimir,

everybody called him Finney—held his livestock
auctions every Friday, attracting farmers from a hundred miles around more or less.

Shortly after the auctions became an established
event, a middle-aged couple, German emigrés,
rented the rundown farm house, made the minimum
repairs necessary, and began selling their homemade
sausages, served hot on fresh-baked buns, and a sour
cream and green apple streusel pie that soon drew
buyers from the nearby town of Lancaster.

With townies on the scene, local farmers began
carting produce to the site on auction day, setting
up tables to display vegetables and fruits as they
came in season, plus preserves, pickles, clover
honey, maple syrup, and home-baked bread and
cakes.

A few began offering pieces of farm equipment
they wanted to dispose of—this was all before garage and yard sales became commonplace—or old
furniture and household junk they no longer wanted.

An antique dealer, out for a drive and the streusel
pie, stumbled onto some really fine old pine pieces.
He paid the ridiculously low prices with a straight
face and let it be known he'd be interested in more
of the same.

The following week he filled a van with the cast-
offs of a dozen old farmsteads. He couldn't resist
bragging to a fellow dealer and the invasion began.

Finney's Farm Flea Market was born.

The T-shirt-and-jeans brigade swiftly followed.

On Fridays the field around the barns became a sea of tables.

Vladimir-Finney, recognizing a money-making opportunity when it blossomed under his nose, started holding the livestock auction on Wednesday and collected rent from the vendors on Friday.

By the time I came to it, the flea market covered an area approximately the size of four city blocks, two thirds of which was paved, the balance in pasture.

There were sharp divisions in the paved section. Three quarters of it was occupied by vendors of new merchandise, who paid a yearly fee for their reserved space.

Most of the vendors in this section had tents and canopies they moved from one outdoor flea market to another, protecting their wares—sweaters, socks, leather jackets, purses, boots, shoes, fabrics, towels, digital watches, spices, pots, pans, cutlery, cheap crystal, tacky ceramic figurines, jewelry, whatever. New junk.

The next three lanes were rented on a first-come basis to the true flea market people, the trash-and-treasure vendors like Rena. And me. Beyond us was the pastureland parking lot, extending from the paved section to the two barns marking the extent of Finney's land.

The old farmhouse was still there but the German couple and their pies were long gone. The house had been expanded with the addition of an ugly cinderblock kitchen where five cooks fired up their grills before dawn and filled orders for fried eggs, fried sausages and pancakes, fried hamburgers, hot dogs, and greasy french fries until dusk.

To the right of the farmhouse, in a lane of permanent stalls running parallel to the highway, was an area reserved for fresh produce. Some of the vendors there actually were farmers, many were not. Their oranges and grapes and eggplant came from the same produce broker who supplied grocery stores in the city.

There was no interrelation between the three categories of vendors. Vendors in our three lanes sometimes ventured into the produce section, particularly when corn was in season, but none of us ever wandered into the new-merchandise section. There was nothing for us there.

THE SKY WAS pearly with dawn, the streetlamps glowing pale orange as I drove through the town of Lancaster, early Friday morning.

I was surprised to find the town had spread almost to Finney's Farm. The old two-lane highway was now four lanes, built up on both sides with an undisciplined hodgepodge of bungalows, car dealerships, two-story flats, beer stores, farm equipment, and feed outlets.

Directly across from the flea market was a vast trailer park sprouting a thicket of television antennas, black and spiky against the rosy horizon.

The rusty farm truck ahead of me veered off into Finney's. I followed it around the farmhouse to find an even more startling sight.

The pastureland of the old parking lot had disappeared under a plateau of tables extending from the paved section clear to the cedar hedge and the barns. There had to be at least four additional lanes of vendors swarming around their vans and pickups and cars, setting up for the day.

Rena's space was on pavement. I crawled up one paved lane and down the next, one eye on the preoccupied dealers rushing left and right and across the back, the other eye searching for space number thirty-five, and for Old Sam.

He'd been watching for me. He stepped out into the lane, waving his arms.

"Back up into here," he called, pointing to his right.

I peered dubiously at the space beside the tables he'd set up in his section.

"I don't know, Sam. I'm not used to this van yet."

"Get out," Old Sam ordered. "I'll do it."

Relieved, I stepped down from the van. Sam hopped in and the van shot back through the narrow passage. With deft maneuvering, he parked it nose-to-nose with his own, establishing a back wall for our combined stalls. He switched off the motor, climbed down from the van and tossed me the keys.

"Slick," I admired. "Thanks, Sam."

"No problem." Old Sam shrugged off my gratitude. "Good to see you again, Catherine. How's Rena doing?"

"She phoned from the hospital last night. Said she felt rotten but she'll live. She asked me if I could come by on Monday, when she's home. I said I would."

"Sounds like Rena." He jerked a thumb at the van. "Need any help unloading?"

"Thanks, no. I'll be okay."

"If you do, holler." He gave me a quick grin and went back to finish his own unpacking.

Old Sam isn't all that old. He's in his early fifties. At one time there was another vendor, considerably younger, also named Sam. To distinguish between them, we referred to one as Old Sam, the other as Young Sam. Young Sam quit flea-marketing several years ago. But habit dies hard. Old Sam is still Old Sam.

I've always liked him. He's a small man, wiry and energetic, with steel gray hair and skeptical, gray eyes the color of murky water. An old scar on his upper lip has left him with a lisp that makes him sound like a stand-up comic doing Humphrey Bogart.

Sliding open the van door, I pulled out Rena's folding metal tables, four of them, and set two up parallel to the lane of traffic and the other two perpendicular to the first pair, so that together with Old Sam's tables they formed a half-square.

I dug out the dark blue bedsheets Rena uses as tablecloths and spread them, clipping the corners against any passing breeze. I unloaded the cartons marked FINNEY'S from the van and began the finicky job of unpacking.

I had unwrapped and set out one Hummel figurine, one large Royal Doulton Toby jug, two Carnival glass bowls, and an ornate Dresden candlestick when suddenly there were five people pressed against the table, one of whom I recognized as Lionel, a hustler who wheels and deals out of the back of his truck. He picked up the Doulton jug, frowning at the price tag.

"Hell, this looks like Rena's ticketing," he muttered. He raised his eyes. "Hey, hello! Long time no see. What's happened to Rena?"

"She's in the hospital. I'm filling in for her."

"She okay? Nothing serious?"

"She's fine. She'll be back."

"Good. Say hello for me." He set the Toby jug down and loped off, back on the prowl for ignorant neophytes and their underpriced treasures.

The other four lingered until I had unpacked the first box. Old hands, they were aware that the first box usually contains anything new a vendor has found during the previous week. Nothing had surfaced they hadn't seen before and they drifted away without buying.

I continued setting up.

Eight years had passed and it was still the same

old same-old. Dishes, books, toys, pots and pans, crocheted doilies and hand-embroidered linens, copper and ceramic planters, a box of fishing lures, a really fine porcelain clock, a music box, some costume jewelry... An eclectic collection of junk, with prices ranging from a dollar for a fairly current paperback book to two hundred for the Royal Doulton Toby jug.

It was six-thirty when I finished.

The morning sun was golden in a blue and cloudless sky, dealers and pickers had departed for greener pastures, sane people were still in their beds, and I was feeling the first pangs of hunger.

Old Sam considered my offer of coffee and a bran muffin with a dubious frown.

"Real coffee? Not instant?" He grimaced. "Or that herbal crap of Rena's that tastes like warm perfume?"

"The coffee's real. So's the muffin. I baked it myself."

I filled the plastic top cup from the thermos and offered it to him.

"You don't have to drink it. I'm only trying to say thanks for holding Rena's place till I got here."

Old Sam's brows lifted. "I didn't save it for you," he said. "It's Rena's. She paid for it." He tasted his coffee. "Ah. That's good, Catherine."

"Thanks. She paid for it? How do you mean? Don't they come around during the day to collect the rent?"

"Oh, sure, they come around and collect." He bit into his muffin. "Rena didn't tell you about the auction?"

"What auction?"

Old Sam held up an admonitory index finger. He chewed and swallowed.

"Three years ago," he said, "that sonofabitch Finney hit on a way to squeeze more money out of the vendors. Spaces on the pavement here are auctioned off for the season. Rena paid two hundred and forty bucks for that spot."

"And she has to pay daily rent on top of that?"

"Bloody right. Plus the permit." Old Sam scowled over the rim of his cup. "When the county decided to widen the road, they figured the flea market should pay for it. They imposed a permit. One hundred and fifty for the season. Or twenty-five bucks per day if you don't buy the permit."

"Is the permit a blue card? I wondered what that was."

"That's it. Keep it handy. A county flunky'll come—"

His words were drowned out by a sudden blast of guitars twanging at an earsplitting pitch. The shattered morning air reverberated for seconds, then the sound dropped to a level where the tune was recognizeable. "Achy Breaky Heart."

I took my hands away from my ears. Old Sam grinned.

"Old Cooley's open for business," he said. "I hope you like 'Achy Breaky Heart.'"

"Cooley? He's still alive?"

Eight years ago, Cooley had been a wizened old man, partially deaf and reputedly dying from some unspecified disease. He sold cassettes, CDs, and various minor items of electronic sound equipment from his booth in the new section.

In sheer self-defense, neighboring vendors had taken to monitoring the volume of his ghetto blaster but they'd been powerless when it came to his program. When Cooley fell in love with a tune, old or new, he played it ragged. Eight years ago he'd been crazy for "My Baby Takes the Morning Train," a song forever associated in my mind with Finney's Farm and the smell of hot pavement, hamburger grease, and sweat.

"You kidding? That stringy old bastard'll outlive our kids." Old Sam handed me his empty cup. "Thanks, Catherine. That hit the spot. You want to take a look-see around before it gets busy?"

"I'd like to. If you don't mind."

"Go ahead. I'll watch your tables for you."

"Thanks, Sam. I won't be long."

"Take your time."

"Half an hour."

THERE WERE SIX LANES, three on pavement, three on sparse grass, each a couple of city blocks in length, Vendors faced one another across an expanse broad enough for two cars to pass comfortably with a few feet to spare.

Avoiding the new-merchandise section—an additional seven lanes—I walked slowly up one lane and down the next, stopping briefly once or twice to say hello to a familiar face. Once off the pavement I was more watchful where I stepped on the rutted, ungraded pastureland.

With the exception of two or three vendors selling hubcaps, a few with rusted garden tools, old records, and ancient *National Geographics,* and a dozen or so others with genuine antiques—overpriced—there was a numbing sameness to the table displays. By the time I reached the end of the last lane I felt I had plodded through a maniacally extended garage sale from which any worthwhile bargain had long since been ferreted out.

I cut between stalls on the way back, partly to avoid trekking back and forth along the endless homogeneity, mostly from a sense of guilt at having been gone too long.

*"Catherine!"*

I turned, scanning for a familiar face, and caught the eyes of a young woman hurrying directly toward me. She was twentyish, slim, and very pretty, with a mane of glossy black hair and very large, very dark eyes.

Her face broke into a radiant smile. I'd never seen her before in my life, and I looked behind me for a reciprocating smile from some other Catherine.

To my astonishment, she threw her arms around
me and gave me a quick, warm hug.

"I knew it was you!" she cried. "You haven't
changed a single day!"

"I haven't?" I said, mystified.

"Not one day." She gestured to a young man
who had followed and stood waiting a few feet
away. "I want you to meet Alex Kalfas. Alex, this
is the Catherine Wilde I've told you about."

I took Alex's extended hand. He had a firm grip,
an engaging smile, a shock of sandy hair, and round
steel-rimmed glasses.

"Look." The young woman tugged at a gold
chain around her neck and pulled a pendant from
under her T-shirt. "I still have it. I wear it all the
time. I love it."

The pendant was a small cameo, no larger than
my thumbnail, distinctive in that it was square in
shape, not the customary oval. The sight of it trig-
gered my memory wheels into swift action.

I deducted eight years in time and four inches in
height, added eighty pounds in weight, a mass of
unkempt hair, a mouthful of braces, and a painfully
adolescent skin.

Eight years ago, here at Finney's, I had given the
cameo as a thirteenth birthday present to a girl who
had borne as much resemblance to this lovely young
woman as a potato dumpling does to spun sugar.
Only the eyes were the same.

"Tina! I'm sorry. I didn't recognize you. You've changed. I mean you've grown up."

Tina giggled. "It's okay. I guess I do look a little bit different. I was a real mess back then, wasn't I?"

"Different, yes. A mess, never." I smiled over a sudden pang of guilt; I'd left Old Sam alone too long. "Listen, I'm sorry, but I have to get back to my table. I'm set up a couple of rows over. Why don't you come by and we'll catch up on each other?"

"We can't." There was genuine regret in her voice. "We only dropped by to see my father. We have to head back to town, and we're running late as it is. Can I call you?"

"Of course. I'm in the book."

"Are you still Mrs. Wilde?"

"What?"

"I mean, you didn't get married again or anything, did you?"

"No." I turned to leave and added, "Nice meeting you, Alex. You look wonderful, Tina."

"Thank you." She gave me a perfect smile. "I'll call!"

Old Sam was embroiled in a low-voiced, heated argument with a grossly obese individual when I returned.

For a moment I wasn't certain it was a man. A loud Hawaiian-print shirt strained across what appeared to be sagging breasts. Green cotton pants were taut over enormous thighs. Kinky red-brown hair formed a corolla around a moon face in which there was no suggestion of the feminine.

His deep-set eyes, pressed like raisins into soft dough, burned with rage under shaggy brows. A neatly trimmed mustache and pointed beard circled an almost lipless slash of mouth. The nose was hawklike, a beak, incongruous in the fleshiness of the bloated face.

He darted only a quick glance at me as I circled the tables. Stabbing a thick finger into Old Sam's chest, he shouted, "Godammit, Sam, I'm telling you now, one more goddamn time and I'm gonna break your goddamn face!"

With curiously graceful steps, he minced to the rear of our booth, squeezed past Old Sam's van and disappeared.

Old Sam delved into his pocket, handed me four dollars. "Sold a pair of salt and pepper shakers for you," he grunted. "The china roosters."

"Thanks." I nodded past him. "You've got customers."

Our day had begun.

# FIVE

WAY BACK in 1914, a man named Sir Walter Raleigh—not the Sir Walter Raleigh of the cape, this one died in 1922—wrote the following lines, apparently while in attendance at a garden party:

> *I wish I loved the Human Race;*
> *I wish I loved its silly face;*
> *I wish I liked the way it walks;*
> *I wish I liked the way it talks....*

Working a flea market like Finney's makes it easy to understand that Victorian gentleman's wistful disenchantment.

There are beautiful human beings in this world. Clean, polite and pleasant and attractive people. The problem at Finney's is they're outnumbered, three to one, by the pig people, a name given to the July-August throngs by a vendor whose own name has long been forgotten.

They're locals and cottagers from the lake district and townies and vacationers up from the city. They arrive in droves, beginning at around ten in the morning, dragging with them their screaming infants, whining toddlers, and surly teenagers. They yank their panting dogs along, oblivious of the effect of sun-baked pavement on unprotected paw pads.

Sitting behind your table, you get an eye-level view of an astounding parade of bare and hairy beer bellies sagging over rump-sprung Levi's, of massive buttocks undulating like jelly in bags of cotton-knit tights, of ill-advised shorts exposing knobbly varicose veins crawling like purple worms up the fish white legs of the elderly, of pubic hair curling around skimpy swim trunks, of anorectic thighs, of male and female genitalia explicitly contoured under painted-on jeans.

A few days at Finney's Farm and I'll bet old Sir Walt wouldn't have been quite as yearning.

As the day progresses and the temperature rises, the adults seem to get ruder and testier, the children louder and crankier.

The sad, suffering dogs simply endure.


By NOON the sun was a glaring eye in the sky. "Achy Breaky Heart" was on its umpteenth replay. I was sweaty, irritable, and in urgent need of a bathroom break.

"Go," Old Sam said. "I'll watch your tables."

I hurried up to the house and stood in line with my legs crossed, nauseated by the greasy cooking odors emanating from the kitchen not more than twenty feet away, and the sharp stink of fake pine disinfectant on the worn linoleum under my feet, thinking, sourly, some things don't change.

Neither do the customers. I had every type at my table through the course of the afternoon.

The lookers—usually matrons checking the price on an article just like the one they have at home. The touchers—mostly finicky little men and artsy-fartsy women with buck teeth and Buster Brown haircuts, who pick up everything on the table and inspect it through a jeweler's loupe, God knows why. The iffers—if it was green... And the knock-ers.

Forget it. I had them all.

I was serving a small, flower-print-clad woman, close to my age, when something odd happened.

She had snatched up a white porcelain pitcher decorated with blue bachelor buttons.

"I remember these!" she crowed. "My mother had the whole set. They used to come in boxes of cereal. Rolled oats! You'd only get one piece at a time, but there were eight of us kids, all eating like horses, and back in those days everybody had hot porridge for breakfast. Not like now, when..."

I tuned her out.

Back in the days when I was doing the markets I felt a certain grudging pity for these elderly women who come to flea markets alone, seeking a captive audience. They're not looking for conversation. They want a human ear into which they can spill their solitary lives.

With no other customers at my tables and no po-lite way to escape, I nodded and smiled and let my eyes wander. They fell on a man heading toward Old Sam.

There was nothing extraordinary about him. He was young—late twenties, I guessed—of medium height, not fat, not thin. His hair was dirty blond, neither long nor short. Several earrings pierced both earlobes. Steel-rimmed John Lennon glasses rested on the bridge of an undistinguished nose, and a two-day stubble sprouted on a weak chin. His sweatshirt read BOSS, his stone-washed jeans were righteously shabby, his sockless feet were Nike shod. If he hadn't been moving with such purposeful intent I would never have noticed him.

He snatched a book from a box of dog-eared paperbacks and thrust it under Old Sam's nose.

"Thirty-five cents," he stated, tentatively belligerent. "Right, Pop?"

Old Sam nodded. Without speaking he took the book. Then, instead of reaching under the table for a bag, he left his customer and went to his van. Startled, I glanced at the young man. He felt my gaze and met it with a flat, hostile stare. I looked away quickly.

Old Sam returned, a yellow plastic bag swinging from his hand. Before passing it across the table, he gestured for payment with an open palm. The young man gave Old Sam a folded wad of bills that couldn't have been any kind of payment for one thirty-five cent paperback, then hurried away.

*"I said, can you do better on the price?"*

I snapped back to my little flower-print lady.

"I'm sorry," I smiled at her. "I was woolgathering."

"Oh, I do it all the time, dear. I'll find myself in the bedroom wondering what it is I came there to get and I have to stop and think back, what was I doing that made me go to the bedroom? Of course, when you get to my age, dear, you tend to be forgetful. Although, actually, it's not so much forgetfulness as having so many things on my mind. These days, it seems to me…"

I took the pitcher from her and checked the tag. Rena had it priced at seven fifty.

"You can have it for six," I said when I could get a word in edgewise. "Six dollars."

She nodded. "I think I'll send it to my sister, Irene. She was the youngest, you know. The hard times, the Depression and all, was mostly over by the time she came along. She probably won't even remember when my mother…"

I stopped listening. There are really only three words a flea market vendor wants to hear.

I'll take it.

By the time I finished wrapping and bagging the pitcher a half dozen browsers were pecking at my table and I was able to cut her short without being unkind. She lingered a moment or two, hopeful, then drifted away.

For the next hour I sold junk, nothing over two dollars. At four o'clock I decided enough was enough and began to pack, toys and books first. They don't have to be wrapped individually. Toss 'em in a box.

"Is this old?"

I looked up from a carton I had finished filling. A young woman, with a baby hanging papoose-style from her shoulders, held a teapot, a very nice cobalt blue pot with heavy silver-deposit trim.

"Fairly old. Sixty, maybe seventy-five years."

"What's the story behind it?"

Story? She wanted a story? I'd give her a story.

"It's English. Made by Sadler. It's a very good piece. And in such fine condition, too." I smiled at her. "I bought it from an eighty-year-old woman who had brought it with her from London when she came here as a war bride."

"Really? Why was she selling it?"

I let the smile fade.

"She was moving into a retirement home and she could only take so much with her, you know? I felt so badly for her. She'd outlived her husband, her children. She had no one. And there I was, buying her precious possessions. It was really very sad."

"Mm," the woman agreed. "Did you say she brought it from London?"

"Yes. She told me it had belonged to her mother."

"Really? Is that your best price?"

"Eighteen?" I hesitated just long enough. "Why don't we say fifteen?"

"I'll take it."

She paid me, and I wrapped it up for her.

"Enjoy it," I said as I handed her the package. "There are a lot of happy memories inside that teapot."

"Mmm," she smiled and sauntered away.

Old Sam had overheard the exchange. He shook his head with mock disapproval.

"Shame on you, Catherine."

I shrugged. "So now the teapot has character. Hey, she got more than her money's worth. That thing was worth three times what she paid."

"Yeah, yeah, I know." Old Sam fanned the air, grinning. "We don't steal. We just lie a lot."

I labored through the packing, schlepped the cartons to the van, broke down the tables, and rammed them into the space behind the passenger seat. It was almost five o'clock when I finished.

I switched on the motor, and while I waited for the air-conditioner to kick in I counted the day's receipts. One hundred thirty-seven dollars and change.

Old Sam waved good-bye. "See you Sunday at Beacon," he called.

On the forty-five minute drive home, as much to keep from dozing as out of curiosity, I worked out the financial statistics.

The summer season at Finney's is approximately

eighteen weeks. Divide the cost of the auction and the price of the permit by eighteen. Add the daily rental, plus gas to-and-from. Take into account what Rena had probably paid for the items I'd sold, roughly one third to one half of what I'd sold them for.

Not counting traveling time, I had worked eleven hours straight for a dollar an hour, give or take a dime.

# SIX

"A BUCK AN HOUR?" Mike's incredulity echoed over the telephone line early the next morning. "Jesus Christ, Cat. That's not even minimum wage."

"I know. But it wasn't a payday weekend. Next week will be better."

"I should hope so. Did you meet up with any of those old buddies you used to bond with?"

"Mike..."

"Okay, okay," he backed off. "Was there anybody you know still around?"

"A few. We said hello, but I didn't stop to chat. Old Sam was watching my tables and I didn't want to push it. I'll probably see them at Beacon tomorrow."

"Beacon?"

"Beacon Mall. The Sunday market."

"Oh. Yeah. Look. Reason I called. How about I take you out for dinner tonight?"

"I'd love to. But I have to be up at five tomorrow morning and I'm still wiped out from yesterday."

"Wiped out? How come?"

"How come? It's damn hard work, Mike, that's how come. Rena was right. I'd forgotten just how much brute labor is involved."

"So quit."

"I can't do that. If Rena loses her spot she'll have to get there the night before to get space in the field. And the field's just a damn cow pasture. If it rains you're standing in puddles and mud. If it doesn't, you're eating dust all day. I can't do that to Rena."

"All right then. No dinner tonight. How about tomorrow? Save you cooking."

"Oh Mike. Same story. When I was doing Beacon eight years ago I never lasted through *Sixty Minutes*."

"What?"

"*Sixty Minutes.* You know. Sunday night? Television? I used to fall asleep halfway through. I don't think I ever saw it straight through the whole time I was doing flea markets. And I was a lot younger then."

There was a pregnant silence. I waited.

"Okay." Mike said with exaggerated patience. "I think maybe I've got it figured out now. No more weekends until your friend—what's her name, Rena? No more weekends until Rena is well enough to take over. Right?"

"That's about the size of it."

"Fine. I'll call you Monday."

"Uh, Mike? Could you make it Tuesday? I have to go to Rena's on Monday."

"Cat... Aaaw, fuck it."

He hung up.

I replaced the receiver. The phone rang immediately and I snatched it up prepared to do battle.

"Hel-lo!" I snapped.

There was a momentary silence, then a woman's hesitant voice said, "Uh…Catherine? Is this Catherine Wilde?"

"Yes," I acknowledged meekly.

"This is Tina Spiridakis. Is this a bad time? Do you want me to call back?"

"No. No. Now's fine. Sorry I barked at you. I thought it was somebody else calling."

"It's okay. Uh…excuse me just a second, Catherine."

I could hear muffled voices, a man's and Tina's, then she was back.

"I'm sorry, Catherine. I'm between classes and I only have a minute, but I wanted to catch you before you go out. Wednesday's my birthday, my twenty-first, and Alex and I are announcing our engagement, so we're having a sort of combined birthday and engagement party, and we'd like you to be there. Can you come?"

The invitation was disconcerting. Parties intimidate me. I scrambled for an easy excuse.

"I really don't like to drive at night, Tina. I mean, any distance…"

"It's at the Casa Grecque. That's not far from you. And dinner is at six—my father likes to eat early. You won't have to drive at night."

"Well…I…"

"Please say you'll come."

"I…" There was no graceful way out. "Would you mind if I skipped dinner? I could drop by about seven-thirty, eight o'clock. Would that be all right?"

"That would be great! I have to run now. I'll see you on Wednesday, then. 'Bye, Catherine."

# SEVEN

BEACON MALL is small as malls go, with a deli at one end and a good bar-restaurant called La Cachette at the other. Between are the usual shops providing services to an upscale neighborhood—florist, dry cleaner, beauty salon, barbershop, optometrist, bookstore, bank, pet store.

The flea market is set up every Sunday in the T-shaped marble-floored center core of the mall, with space to comfortably accommodate a maximum of twenty-five vendors. The market is advertised as an "old-fashioned" flea market, with some justification.

There are no T-shirts for sale. No jeans. With the exception of vintage articles, the selling of clothing is prohibited. There are no baseball cards, no knock-off perfumes, no handicrafts. Other than an occasional piece tucked in discreetly with the old, any display of new merchandise is discouraged. There are no hot dog stands, no doughnut stalls. The only food available is from the delicatessen or from La Cachette.

Compared to Finney's, Beacon is an easy day. The mall is air-conditioned, the washrooms clean and adequate. Spaces are reserved for vendors who are, if not friends, at least amiable acquaintances of long standing. Most have been setting up at Beacon, summer and winter, since the flea market's inception eighteen years ago.

It's the oldest flea market in town, with a long list of vendors waiting for space. If Rena was forced out now she would probably have to wait a lot longer than a year to get back in, which would be disastrous for her. Beacon is her main source of income.

I ARRIVED TO the normal organized confusion occurring when the doors to the mall are thrown open. Beacon's single disadvantage is that cars and vans must be abandoned in the parking lot and everything—folding tables, furniture and cartons—must be carried into the mall.

A few vendors use dollies, ungainly in summer, hopeless in winter snow. Most, like me, plod back and forth from car to mall, observing the vendor's unwritten law—the person carrying has the right of way at the entrances.

Inside, the mall looked and sounded like an angry beehive, the aisles crowded with burdened vendors complaining and pushing past knots of antique dealers and pickers ferreting into cartons still unpacked. The air thrummed with the steady babble of greetings, of queries, of lame humor. Metal tables screeched on marble as they were pushed into position.

Old Sam caught sight of me and waved me to the space directly across from his. "That's Rena's," he called. "Need any help?"

"Thanks, Sam. I'll be okay."

There was a sudden crash, the unmistakable sound of china shattering, followed by a dead silence.

"Was it expensive?" a sympathetic voice cried out.

"No," came the reply from farther down the mall.

"One down, two to go," someone sang out, referring to the vendor's superstition that breakage comes in threes.

The clamor and bustle immediately picked up again. I dodged a trolley and went back outside to the van for the last carton marked BEACON.

I had carried in all four tables, forgetting that the area alloted each vendor was smaller than at Finney's. Mildly annoyed—I'd have to carry the fourth back to the van—I kicked open the three tables and set them up one across, two perpandicular at either end of the first, forming a shallow U, and began unpacking.

For twenty frantic minutes I unwrapped directly into the greedy hands of dealers pressed against my table. I dickered dealer discounts, sold, wrapped, bagged, took cash and made change, explained Rena's absence repeatedly, greeted a few familiar faces...

As abruptly as it had begun, the rush was over. The dealers, recognizing the contents of the third carton, vanished, and I was able to finish setting up at a more leisurely pace.

By nine-thirty the flea market had settled in for the day. The noise level fell to a hum of conversation pitched barely above the music emanating from a vendor's radio.

Two or three dealers, relaxed now the cream had been skimmed, lingered to shmooze. Five or six early risers, regulars with nothing better to do on a Sunday morning, drifted aimlessly from table to table, kibitzing with the vendors. They would dawdle, buying nothing, until La Cachette opened its doors, then treat themselves to a lavish brunch.

Taking advantage of the lull, I went for a stroll, leaving my tables unattended, something unheard of at any other flea market. There is no record of thievery at Beacon. Vendors watch out for one another and the morning regulars are old friends.

At Beacon, vendors try for the beautiful, the old, and the unusual. They bring their best. On any given Sunday you might find a Dresden figurine, a Guttman print from the thirties in its original frame, an old cast-iron mechanical bank or a celluloid kewpie doll among the standard flea market merchandise.

In addition to their bread-and-butter items, a few of the vendors drift into specifics. Old Sam has display cases of estate jewelry and old pocket watches. Phil and Laura, a couple in their seventies, are able to identify Carnival and Depression glass reproductions from ten feet away. Mark specializes in old clocks, Norman in primitives, Elsa in Hummels.

They all asked about Rena. I assured them she was fine and would be back soon and continued down the mall.

Turning the corner into the crossbar of the T, I found Old Sam sipping coffee from a plastic cup and scowling down at a vendor's table situated across from the deli. There was no one behind the table.

"Look at this stuff," he muttered, encircling my arm with his free hand. "Take a good look."

I looked, then looked again. I picked up an exquisitely carved ivory fan. It was genuine ivory. I tilted a figurine I thought might be Meissen and found the blue crossed swords on the bottom. An Art Nouveau calling-card tray that looked like sterling *was* sterling. A small blue and gold rouge pot with a hand-painted medallion of a pale woman in a powdered wig was Sèsvres. A glass boudoir clock mounted in an onyx frame was signed R. Lalique.

"Wow. Whose stuff is this?"

"Brady's."

"Who is Brady?"

"New guy." Old Sam's mouth turned down with distaste. "He's a punk smart-ass. Been in it a few months and thinks he knows it all."

"He must know something." I picked up a fragile

basket woven of opalescent porcelain. It was Belleek. "Where's he getting pieces like this?"

"That's what I'd like to know."

"Why don't you ask him?"

"He says auctions, but that's a crock." Old Sam's eyes narrowed. "Hold it. Here he comes."

Threading his way toward us was a tall, very thin man, slightly stoop shouldered. His walk was almost ungainly, as though his arms and legs operated on unconnected circuits. His long, brown hair, parted in the center, fell around a narrow, somehow ascetic face. His beard was neatly trimmed.

"Looks like Jesus H. Christ?" I asked.

"That's him." Old Sam pressed my arm, steering me away from the table. "Thinks he's Jesus H. Christ too."

We walked slowly back to our spots at the base of the T.

"So you don't believe he's getting all that beautiful stuff at auction?" I asked.

Old Sam grimaced. "I bloody well know he isn't. I go to the same auctions. I go to all the viewings. You don't think I'd have spotted something like that sterling W. M. F. Tray? Or the Sèvres?"

"Maybe he's found a secret source. Maybe he does a lot of running."

"Hell, I do a lot of running. Where's he running?"

"Ask him."

Old Sam snorted. "Yeah. Sure. He's going to tell me."

"So follow him." It was a fatuous suggestion and I made it lightly. To my surprise, Old Sam stopped dead in his tracks and eyed me thoughtfully.

"You know," he said, "I might just do that."

"Come on, Sam," I began, and would have probably followed through with some idiotic attempt at humor if I hadn't seen Mike limping toward us, a sheepish grin on his face.

"Hey! Cat! I finally found the goddamn place."

"You're a genius. What are you doing here?"

"Muhammad and the mountain," he said cheerfully. "I figured if I'm going to see you at all this summer it'll have to be in one of these schlock houses."

He glanced at Old Sam, then looked again, more closely. "I know you from somewhere don't I? Have we met?"

Old Sam shook his head. "I doubt it."

"Sam. Mike." I gestured from one to the other.

They shook hands, Mike frowning, then Old Sam withdrew his hand. "Sorry." He gestured at his table. "Customers."

There were two women at my own table. I went to serve them, Mike trailing behind. He waited patiently as I wrapped their purchases, attended to a couple requesting information on an Eskimo carving, and refused too low an offer on a Steiff bear.

"Now," he said when they had all moved on.

"How about I buy you brunch in La Cachette there."

"I can't, Mike. It's starting to get busy. I can't leave my tables."

"How about lunch, then, later? You have to eat."

"I bring my lunch. I eat it right here." Seeing storm clouds gathering, I added hastily, "Why don't you come for dinner on Tuesday? I'll make lasagna just for you."

Mike's face relaxed into a broad grin. "I thought you'd never ask. Okay. Mission accomplished. I guess I can take off now."

"Aren't you going to look around?"

"Look around?" he said blankly. "At what?"

I laughed. He meant it, he really did.

"Okay, Mike. See you Tuesday."

UNLIKE THE motley assortment at Finney's, the Beacon crowd falls into distinct groups.

Many are middle-aged or retired—couples and widows and widowers—who established their Sunday outing routine years ago. Church first, on to brunch at La Cachette, then an hour or two browsing through the flea market, visiting with those vendors they've come to know by name.

They're well dressed. They're polite. They're pleasant. They buy selectively, often for their children and their grandchildren. They play the game of haggling with great good humor, delighted with even a token discount.

Then there are the thirty-somethings, mostly young couples, both with careers. Some are fledgling collectors, others are homeowners looking for unusual items to enhance their decor. They cruise the weekend flea markets. When they find what they're after, they spend freely.

And then there are the rest of them.

The twenty-year-olds looking for toasters for their first apartments. Young mothers buying recycled toys. The first-time flea-market visitors, agog at what they see. They're fun. We even instruct them on how to haggle successfully. There are the cheapos, who want everything at half the marked price. They're not fun. We don't haggle with them at all.

And finally, inescapably, the boors. Fortunately, a lot fewer than at Finney's.

Mine came in the afternoon, a group of four. Two pudgy men and their matronly wives.

The mall acoustics are tricky. The ceiling is domed. On occasion a conversation twenty feet away will be heard more clearly than words spoken across the table.

The foursome paused inside the door. One of the men, a pasty-faced type wearing heavy glasses, laid down the law.

"Okay." He stabbed a fat finger at the others. "Let me do the talking. I know how to handle these people."

These people. Oh boy.

They inspected Old Sam's table, then approached mine.

One of the women snatched up a large porcelain flower arrangement, cooing to her husband. Pasty Face snapped his fingers to get my attention.

"She likes it," he said. "I'll give you twenty bucks."

"I'm sorry. It's marked thirty-eight dollars."

He reached for his wallet, withdrew a twenty, and snapped it three inches from my nose.

"Twenty." He waved the bill. "Cash."

"Sorry." I pushed his arm aside. "But I'll tell you what I'll do for you. Come back in half an hour. Pack up all this stuff, load it into my van and I'll give you the flowers for nothing."

His eyes turned mean.

"Lady," he snapped, "you're nuts."

I watched them march away, then looked at the tables surrounding me.

Man, I thought, you are so right.

# EIGHT

On Monday morning I called Rena and told her I'd be at her place around ten-thirty.

Lucie met me at the door and led me into the kitchen, where Rena, wrapped in a blue terry robe, sat in her favorite pressback chair. She looked wan and slightly frayed around the edges.

"How are you feeling?" I asked.

"The way I expected to feel." She waved that subject aside. "How about you? How did it go?"

"Just fine."

"Before you two get down to business..." Lucie set a small pitcher on the table. "Here's the milk. Tea's ready. I'd better get back upstairs before Brandon drives my auntie up the wall." She flashed her impish gap-toothed grin at me. "Nice seeing you again, Catherine."

"You too, Lucie."

She touched Rena's shoulder in passing, "Call me if you need anything," she said, and was gone.

"So. Tell me." Rena filled two mugs with tea and pushed one toward me.

I handed her a list of the articles I had sold and an envelope containing her money.

"Finney's wasn't great. Beacon was better." I

sniffed at my mug. It wasn't the herbal tea Old Sam had complained of. I added milk. "I was surprised at how many new vendors there are at Finney's."

Rena, scanning her list, nodded. "The recession."

"And a lot of the old ones are gone. I didn't see Pete and Pitou, for instance, not at either market. They used to do both, didn't they?"

"Pitou died of AIDS. Two years ago." Rena set the list aside and sipped her tea. "Nobody seems to know what happened to Pete. He just disappeared."

"What about the Georges? Saint George and Shifty George?"

Rena grimaced. "Saint George won a lot of money in one of the lottos. He moved away to California to start a new religion."

I snickered. It was difficult to imagine the Saint George we knew acquiring followers. He was a sanctimonious toad of a man with a piercing, ground-glass voice. When Saint George spoke, people cringed.

"What about Shifty George. I didn't see him either."

"He's out of business. Maybe a month ago the police came to Finney's and seized his stock."

"Why?"

"The story is he was dealing in stolen goods."

"Was he?"

"I don't know. I don't pay attention. Maybe yes, maybe no. It is possible. There were always not-so-nice people visiting George. You remember."

I nodded. "I remember. And speaking of not-so-nice people, Old Sam had some kind of set-to at Finney's. Big man, fat, lots of kinky reddish hair. Do you know him?"

"He had a pointy beard? His name is Leo. He deals out of his pockets. I don't like him. He can be very nasty."

"He was being very nasty with Old Sam."

"Well…" Rena's mouth tightened. "Sam can be very nasty himself. He has taken a dislike to one of the newer vendors, and he is making the boy miserable."

"Are you talking about a vendor named Brady? Tall, long brown hair?"

Rena's face brightened. "You met Brady?"

"He was at Beacon yesterday. I saw his table. He has some very impressive pieces. But this Brady is no boy, if he's the vendor you mean. I figured him at least thirty-five or forty."

"Thirty-six." Rena said. "Maybe I think of him as a boy because he was so sort of helpless when he started. He was set up next to me at Old Port."

"You do the Old Port flea market?"

"Every so often. To get rid of junk. Brady was next to me. He had a few good pieces, too much underpriced. I told him he should ask five times as much for them. They all sold at the prices I suggested. He was very grateful."

"He should be," I snorted. "Any other vendor

would have bought the pieces from him and sold them just as easily at five times what they paid him.''

"I know. But I could not do it, Catherine. He lost his job. He has a wife and two children. His wife had inherited the good pieces from her grandmother and he told me it killed him to have to sell them.''

"If his wife inherited the pieces I saw on his table yesterday, that was some kind of grandmother she had.''

"The grandmother's things only started him off,'' Rena said. "They went right away.''

"So where's he getting all that good stuff?''

"He runs,'' Rena said earnestly. "To every garage sale, house sale, estate sale, every auction sale. Whatever and wherever. He works hard, Catherine.''

"Sounds as if you like him.''

"I do,'' Rena said firmly. "He is a nice person. He is polite. He is helpful. He is a good man.''

"If you say so.'' I pushed Brady aside, together with my empty tea mug. "What about stock, Rena? I didn't sell much at Finney's, but I'll need something new for Beacon.''

Rena shook her head.

"Please,'' she said. "I wish you wouldn't worry about selling. It doesn't matter if you sell. It is only important that you keep my spaces.''

"That's what I'm doing,'' I said, getting up to put the milk pitcher in the fridge. "But if I'm sitting there I may as well be making money for you. Even one new box would be better than nothing.''

"Next week. This week, maybe go with what you have and I will put together more for next week.''

"It's your party.'' I carried the mugs to the sink.

"You know, Rena,'' I said as I went back to the table and sat down. "Something peculiar happened at Finney's.''

"What?'' Rena was tiring. She leaned heavily on her elbows.

"I saw a customer give Old Sam a wad of folding money for a thirty-five-cent paperback. Really strange.''

Rena had stiffened as I spoke. She looked at me with shuttered eyes. "So?''

"So...well...'' I stumbled, taken aback at the hostility in her voice. "I just thought you might know what that was all about.''

"No,'' she said stonily. "I do not.'' Her gaze slid away from my face.

"Well...'' I stood up, mystified. She was obviously lying and doing it badly. "Maybe it was my imagination. Is there anything I can do for you before I leave?''

"Thank you, no. I think I will lie down for a while.''

"Good idea. I'll call you next Monday, okay?'' She began to rise from her chair but I waved her back into it. "Don't get up. I know the way out.''

I was on my way out the kitchen door when she spoke my name. I turned.

"Thank you, Catherine," she said. Two spots of color burned on her pale cheeks. "I appreciate your help."

"No problem."

I DROVE HOME, muttering to myself.

I hate people who use bankrupt phrases like *no problem* as universal catchalls. And here I am, doing it myself.

I hate what I can't stop myself from thinking—that Old Sam is involved in something illegal.

Most of all, I hate feeling like an Avon lady who has just had the door slammed in her face.

Dammit, Rena, I thought we were friends.

# NINE

THE NEXT MORNING while I was eating breakfast and doing the *New York Times* crossword puzzle, my daily Alzheimer's check, the phone shrilled. I picked it up and Charlie Harwood's voice blasted in my ear.

"Cat! Where the hell have you been?"

"Hello, Charlie. How's it going?"

"Same shit, different day," he said, losing a couple decibels. "You still in business? I've been trying to get you for four days. Where the hell have you been?"

"I've been flea-marketing." I took a bite of toast.

"What do you mean, flea-marketing?" A sharper note crept into his voice. "Buying or selling?"

"Selling." I chewed hastily and swallowed.

"Selling? Cat, you wouldn't be selling without letting us get first—"

"No, Charlie, I wouldn't," I interrupted. "It's a long story and I'll tell it to you some day when we have nothing better to talk about. What can I do for you?"

"We picked up an early Victorian rosewood sewing table the other day. Some insensitive arse kept a plant on it. Left a white ring on the top."

"Early Victorian? Does it have a workbag?"

Old sewing tables often have a cloth workbag hanging underneath. I've always thought the bags look like udders but what do I know?

"The bag is in tatters."

"They always are."

"Can you replace it?"

"What kind of fabric is it?"

"Ivory damask. Rafe says it's pure silk."

"If you're not in a rush I could probably track some down. It might take a little time, though."

"Whatever."

"I can't pick it up today, Charlie. I'm finishing a chest I promised delivery on tomorrow afternoon. I can pass by your place on my way home. That be okay?"

"We can do better. We're going to a viewing on the lakeshore tonight. We'll drop it off."

"Great. Charlie? Why don't you and Rafe plan to have dinner here. Mike's coming."

"Uh, what are you having?"

I blew out an exasperated breath.

"Charlie. Every time I invite you to dinner you ask me the same dumb question. Do you do that to everybody?"

"No," Charlie responded cheerfully. "Only you."

"Oh? Why only me?"

"Only you, because the chili you once made was so goddamn hot it gave me the worst case of hemorrhoids I've ever had in my life. You're a good cook, Kitty Cat, but I have to tell you, your chili's a pain in the ass."

I stifled the impulse to laugh. "I'm sorry, Charlie," I said contritely. "No chili. I'm making lasagna."

"Hold on a sec."

I could hear the murmur of Charlie's voice and Rafe's response, then Charlie was back.

"Cat? Sounds good. But we'll have to eat fairly early. The viewing is scheduled for eight o'clock."

"So we'll eat at six."

"Want us to bring anything?"

"Just yourselves. And the work table, of course."

"Sho 'nuff. See you later," Charlie said, and hung up.

I went back to work on the chest without enthusiasm.

Restoring furniture, as I do, can be a pleasurable way to earn a living. Stripping varnish stain blackened by age to find beautiful old wood hidden underneath can be a thrill. Okay, a small thrill, but gratifying nonetheless.

There was no satisfaction in this chest.

It was an abortion of veneer over birchwood, with three drawers; one bowed, the other two flat. It had clumsy bun feet and garlands of tacked-on brass roses.

I was working on it for my least favorite client, an interior decorator named DeeDee Janns, who would overprice it and unload it on one of her clients as old and quaint, a period piece.

It was, undisputably, a period piece. But it had been third-rate junk ninety years ago and age hadn't improved its status. Now it was old junk.

Antiques are like people. Good breeding and good bones are a joy forever. Schlock remains schlock to the bitter end.

# TEN

THEY ARRIVED simultaneously, Mike with a gloriously blooming azalea plant and a bottle of chianti, Rafe carrying the sewing table.

Charlie, as always, made an entrance. It is impossible for Charlie to simply walk into a room. He sweeps all before him.

Charlie is impressive, Charlie is a presence. He's over six feet tall, he's over sixty years old and looks fifty. And he hasn't gained an ounce since his college football days.

A precisely trimmed salt-and-pepper Vandyke beard masks a misshapen jaw, his legacy from a gang of gay-bashing drunks. A black velvet patch hides the empty socket of his missing left eye. The remaining eye is a wicked, pale hazel.

When he came out of the closet he reinvented himself, leaving printing salesman Charlie Harwood behind, becoming the Charles Harwood of exclusive, prestigious—and pricey—Canterbury House Antiques. He wears Edwardian jackets, always with a fresh rosebud in the lapel, white silk turtlenecks, lean trousers. He has honed to perfection a public image of lofty hauteur. In private, he's a bustling, irreverent old sweetie pie.

Rafe is Rafael Verdoni, with a profile straight from an ancient Roman coin. When you see him head on, the illusion shatters. The left side of his face was destroyed by the same yahoos who disfigured Charlie. Heavy scarring and frozen musculature have left him with a lopsided smile. That enigmatic smile, his lean, feline grace, and the lush velour clothing he designs for himself lend him an aura of the exotic.

He's ten years younger than Charlie. He's also ten times smarter—a fact Charlie happily acknowledges. Rafe is Canterbury House's brain, Charlie its elegant body.

In contrast, Mike and I are like scruffy, aging peasants. Mike has the wrinkled, slightly frazzled look of a man with no sartorial vanity whatsoever. His pate is balding, a potbelly slowly evolving.

I spend most of my waking hours in T-shirts and jeans. I was never a beauty, so the signs of age creeping up don't bother me too much. I look into a mirror in the morning when I put on makeup and assure myself wrinkles are character lines. I earned them all.

A few things, like bosom and butt, are starting to sag. Oh, well. Like everyone over sixty—except Charlie—I'm fighting the inevitable downward pull of gravity.

"Hey, Cat." Charlie waved a videocassette in the air. "We brought you a wee giftie."

"What is it?" I took the cassette from him and

read the title: *The Adventures of Priscilla, Queen of the Desert.* "Priscilla! I've seen it three times. I love it!"

"I knew you would." Charlie took a seat at the kitchen table, already set for dinner. "How about Terence Stamp? Was he incredible or what? That *face!*"

"The scene with the Maoris."

"The kid on top of the bus with the flying banners."

"Where was the baggage?" Rafe pulled out a chair across from Charlie. "Where was the baggage when the kid was on top of the bus?"

"What? Who cares where the baggage was?"

"Just wondering," Rafe said mildly.

"For Christ's sake, Rafe!" Charlie roared. "Don't be so bloody literal-minded."

"Hold it." Mike's head had swivelled back and forth like a tennis match spectator's. "Who is Priscilla?"

"Priscilla is a bus." I handed Mike a corkscrew. "Here. Open your chianti."

"Priscilla," Charlie elaborated, "is a bus crossing the Australian outback with three gay performers on their way to a gig in Alice Springs."

"Wow," Mike's brows rose. "A real cliff hanger."

"Don't knock it," I protested. I removed the pan of lasagna from the oven and carried it to the table. "Priscilla is my all-time-best feel-good movie."

Which led to a sometimes heated discussion of favorite movies, with Charlie opting for *Casablanca*—"What can I tell you? I'm a romantic"— Mike for *Godfathers I* and *II*—"Not Three, that was total disaster"—Rafe for *Deliverance*—"The best horror-suspense film ever made."

"*Deliverance?* Come on," Charlie scoffed. "What about *Silence of the Lambs?*"

"Too contrived," Mike said. "A situation has to be within the realm of plausible possibility to inspire true horror. *Misery* did it better."

"*Misery?*" Charlie turned on him. "Which one's that?"

"The crazy broad holding the writer captive."

"Balls it was better. You thought so because you related to the main character."

"He wrote romance novels. I'm not that kind of writer."

"You're not James Caan either."

"How about *Psycho?*" I put in my two cents' worth. "I saw it thirty-something years ago and I still get the occasional nervous twinge in the shower. That's horror."

"That's paranoia," Rafe said. "Compared to *Deliverance*, one thumb up."

Everybody's a critic.

"THAT WAS GOOD, Cat." Charlie pushed aside his empty plate. "So. What's the long story? Why are you doing the flea markets again?"

I explained Rena's predicament.

"She'd lose Beacon. And sleeping in a van at Finney's just to get a spot..." I shrugged.

"She wouldn't do much sleeping," Charlie said. "Dealers run around with flashlights all night. Nobody sleeps. How long are you stuck with it?"

"Five weeks, maybe six."

Charlie's brow lifted. "Well, time flies when you're having fun." His yellow eye glinted. "You having fun?"

The question took me by surprise. Fun? I shook my head.

"I don't think anybody's having fun anymore."

"What d'you mean?"

"I'm not sure. The atmosphere...the mood? It's not the same. Back then"—I waved a hand at eight years past—"most of the vendors were older couples, trying to get by until their old-age pensions kicked in. Or supplementing pensions that were set up when a dollar was worth more than twenty cents. I'm not saying they had fun, but there was a certain good-natured...kinship? Comradeship?"

"Bonding?" Mike said.

"Now," I went on, ignoring him, "there are ten times as many vendors, and some of them are pretty rough-looking. There's something, I don't know, *predatory* about them. They don't smile. Even the old-timers I said hello to struck me as wary. It's all changed. There's an undercurrent I can't put my finger on, but I feel it. As if everything could turn nasty very fast.''

Rafe had been listening quietly. Now he said, ''Nothing has changed, Cat. It was always that way.''

''Not as I remember it,'' I protested.

''You sold at flea markets for how long? Two summers?''

''Two summers, one winter. A year and a half.''

''You were selling off the junk that was in this house when you bought it. And when it was all gone, you quit.''

''So?''

''So you weren't a threat to anybody.''

''How do you mean, a threat? Who to?''

''The vendors who scramble for something new to sell, week after week. They didn't have to beat you out at garage sales. You were never ahead of them in the line waiting to get into an estate sale. You were never in anybody's way, so you were never exposed to the flip side.''

''The flip side?''

''The dark and dirty. We're talking livelihoods here, Cat. You never had to sell to eat, so you really have no conception of the nasty things people will do for the money they need to keep going.''

My suspicions about Old Sam flashed into my head. Before I could voice them, Charlie scraped his chair back from the table and leapt to his feet.

"Shit. Look at the time," he said. "We're going to be effing late. Sorry, Cat, we hate to eat and run. The lasagna was great. Come on, Rafe."

I went with them to the door and waved them off. Mike was smoking a cigarette and staring down at his shoes with a bemused expression when I returned to the kitchen.

I poured two cups of coffee, placed one in front of him, and sat down opposite with mine, saying nothing. He felt my gaze and glanced up.

"What?" he demanded, frowning.

"That's what I want to know."

"What d'you mean?"

"You've been snapping my head off. You walked out on me. You hung up on me. You brought me a plant." I touched one of the bright azalea blossoms. "Something you've never done before. You brought a bottle of wine. Also something you've never done before. So what I'm asking is, what?"

Mike stubbed his cigarette in the ashtray. He stirred the ashes with the dead butt.

"Intimations of mortality," he said finally. "I've had a few bad tachycardia attacks lately."

"You said the doctors told you tachycardia isn't fatal."

"Yeah, yeah. That's what they told me," Mike said sourly. "But when you're laid out like a beached whale, with a vise clamped on your throat and your heart thudding double-time for four hours, you start having a few doubts as to whether those arrogant pricks know what they're talking about.''

"Are you taking your pills?"

"Of course I'm taking my pills," Mike snapped. "I'm not stupid. They're just not working."

"So tell your doctor. Have you been to see him since he gave you the prescription?"

"No. What the hell for?"

"Mike, that was almost two years ago. Dammit, Mike," I said, exasperated. "You're right. You're not stupid. But there are times when you're just plain jackass stubborn."

I snatched up the two mugs, went to the sink, and poured the coffee down the drain.

"You're drinking too much coffee," I snapped.

"Jackass stubborn?"

We glared at one another across the room, then Mike grinned that dumb clown's grin of his. I refilled the mugs and carried them to the table and sat down.

"Intimations of mortality?" I prompted.

Mike lit another cigarette. He inhaled deeply, blew out a thin stream of smoke, and watched it disperse into a blue-gray haze above our heads.

"When you're lying there, Cat," he began thoughtfully, "waiting for your pulse to click back into gear, your mind begins to wander in strange and fanciful ways."

He poked his chest with his forefinger.

"You have this machine in here," he said. "It

squishes blood back and forth, or whatever. This piece of equipment starts up when they yank you away from your mother and smack your bare baby bottom. And it never stops. Think about it, Cat. What other machine is there that flub-dubs along for sixty years, night and day, without ever being switched off, without ever being overhauled?''

I nodded. ''Go on.''

''You begin to realize, hey, this motor could blow up in the next six days, in the next six months. It has one hell of a lot of miles on it. So I'm lying there and I'm thinking, this could be my last summer.''

''It won't be. The tachycardia isn't going to kill you. The cigarettes, maybe, but not the tachycardia.''

''God,'' Mike snorted, ''you're a real pain in the butt since you quit. Haven't you ever heard that old saying, there's nothing so righteous as a whore on her day off?''

I burst out laughing. In spite of himself, Mike smiled.

''Anyway,'' he said, ''I'd be lying there, vibrating like a hooked trout and getting mad as hell at you.''

''At me? Why me?''

''Because you were ruining my last and final summer.'' Mike raised his hand to forestall any protest. ''I told you, Cat, when you're riding out an attack, you get maudlin. I could see the summer stretching ahead and I felt abandoned. I hate to admit it, but I miss you.''

"Well..." I was at a loss. Mike, ordinarily, is about as sentimental as the IRS. "I guess a little bit of maudlin never hurt anybody. I miss you too.''

"What's the name of that flea market you're doing on Friday?''

"Finney's. Why?''

"I think I'll go out there this Friday.''

"Mike. I'm touched.''

"Don't get too touched. I want another look at that Sam of yours. I know I've met him, whatever he says. And until I figure out when and where, it'll drive me crazy.''

"Speaking of Old Sam..." I told Mike about the transaction at Finney's.

"You didn't see how much the guy paid?'' he asked.

"The top bill was a ten,'' I said. "I couldn't see the rest, but I'm positive Old Sam counted four bills.''

"What about Sunday? The other flea market? Same thing there?''

"No.'' I thought a moment. "But the box of paperbacks wasn't on Old Sam's table at Beacon.''

Mike blew out a cloud of smoke and squinted through it. "You think he may be selling drugs, don't you,'' he said.

"I don't know what to think. I like Old Sam. I find it hard to believe he might be a drug dealer.

But you heard what Rafe said. People do nasty things for money. And if you're slick about it, I suppose a flea market could be a good place to peddle drugs. I don't remember ever seeing any police around. At least, not in uniform.''

"What about this friend of yours? Rena? Do you think she might know what it's all about?''

"I asked her. She said not. But she was lying.''

"Uh,'' Mike grunted. "So what are you going to do?''

"I don't know. Keep watching?''

"And if what you suspect turns out to be true?''

I shrugged. "I don't know. Probably nothing. But I'll sure as hell be disenchanted with Old Sam.''

# ELEVEN

OTHER THAN trips to the grocery store and the hardware store, I rarely go out to shop. Clothes no longer interest me. I'm content and comfortable with my collection of unmatched, garage-sale sofas and chairs and tables and lamps, and I have no aching need to update or replace them. If I go to a mall it's usually for a specific item. I buy and get out.

So I was feeling mildly resentful and put-upon next morning as I trudged past shop after shop in the vast, bright shopping mall with its central island of trees soaring two levels high.

What do you buy for a young woman, a stranger, on the occasion of her twenty-first birthday? Not jewelry. At sixteen, my daughter Laurie had informed me my taste was archaic. Clothing, same deal. Books? More of the same.

After cruising for almost two hours, I sat down on a marble bench, tired and frustrated, and stared vacantly at the gift shop facing me.

Sunlight streamed down through the lofty skylight and filtered through the quivering leaves above, striking a display in the shop window. A rainbow flashed.

I leapt up and hurried into the shop. Five minutes

later I was on my way, seventy dollars poorer, with the perfect gift nestled in tissue inside a silver box.

A Swarovski crystal butterfly.

EIGHT YEARS AGO.

It was early in July on a warm and windy day at Finney's Farm. Empty chip bags, candy wrappers, and wadded-up balls of Kleenex bounced down the lanes, occasionally whipped up onto our tables by dust devils.

A small sheet of rose-colored writing paper was flipped into my lap. Two more fluttered to rest on my table. I gathered the three sheets and idly scanned them.

There was a poem on each page, carefully hand-written in a lurid shade of purple ink. They were the yearning, awkward poems of an adolescent. The kind of poetry I wrote when I was twelve, that Laurie wrote and hid from me.

I read the last two lines of the final poem, then reread them, captivated.

*And on that day I will soar to the sky,*
  *On the wings of a sun-struck butterfly.*

"Excuse me," a timid voice ventured. "Those are mine."

I looked up.

A young girl with a tangled mane of frizzy black hair leaned against my table, peering at me.

Clutched against her bosom were more of the rosy sheets.

I handed her the three pages. "Did you write them?"

The girl's fist tightened on her poems. Her shoulders hunched protectively and she mumbled something I assumed to be an admission of guilt. She reached out and snatched the pages from me.

"They're good," I said, and quoted the two butterfly lines. "I think that's beautiful."

"You do? Really?" Her face blossomed into a steel-retainer smile. She instantly covered her mouth with her hand, a self-conscious gesture that took me right back to the days when Laurie wore the detested braces on her teeth.

"Really," I assured her. "Sun-struck butterfly, that's a lovely image."

She pushed the riot of hair back from her face. Her eyes were blue-white with health, the irises a rich chocolate.

"Do you…would you like to read the rest?" she asked, smiling shyly.

"Well…" I indicated waiting customers. Her face fell. "What's your name?" I added hastily.

"Tina."

"Are you a vendor? I mean, are you here with a vendor?"

"With my father." She flapped a hand. "He's set up down there."

"Okay, Tina. Let's do it this way. Leave the poems with me now and come back at noon, when it's

quieter. Bring your lunch with you. We'll eat together and talk about them. How does that sound?''

This time she made no attempt to hide her smile.
She surrendered her poems, initiating the ritual that
was to continue throughout the summer, my last at
Finney's Farm.

She was like a damp puppy that summer. Baby-
fat pudgy and awkward, with constant moisture in
the corners of her mouth and eyes and at her hair-
line. A rash of adolescent pimples inflamed her forehead and chin, and she picked at them with bitten
fingernails. If she owned clothes other than the faded
lavender T-shirt and cutoff jeans she had on the day
we met, I never saw them.

Her poems were emotional outpourings, youth-
fully sweet and sad. And derivative. No more sun-
struck butterflies. She dropped them off early in the
morning and returned at noon for lunch and a sem-
inar.

I corrected her spelling and added punctuation—
hers was nonexistent. I scribbled a random *good* or
*I like this* on the pink pages and smiled and nodded
at impassioned explanations of her transparent im-
ages.

After our second session together I walked her
back to her father's setup to reassure him she was
spending her lunch hour in friendly territory.

He was a new vendor, a man I'd never seen before.

His tables were laden with restaurant-type china
and glassware, shiny stainless steel kitchen equip-

ment—coffee urns, deep fryers, great soup pots, pans, cutting boards, knives of every size—stacks of white linen tablecloths and napkins, a pile of large metal trays, and box upon box of silver-plated flatware.

A row of dark oak barstools with padded red leather seats marked the perimeter of his space. Several pedestal tables had been upended and set one on top of the other. At least a dozen Tiffany-style hanging lamps littered any free ground area, leaving nowhere to sit and barely room to move.

"Poppa?" Tina wriggled her way to where her father was wrapping and packing bar stemware for a waiting customer. "This is my friend. This is Catherine."

He glanced up and across at me.

"Don't let her be a nuisance," he said, and returned his attention to his busy hands.

"I won't." I smiled at Tina. "See you next week."

I walked back to my tables, mildly curious. So Tina's father was a gray-haired man with an abrupt manner, a large nose, and the darkest, saddest eyes I'd ever seen.

On the third Tuesday, an oppressively hot and humid day, as I braided her hair to get it off her face, Tina proudly informed me she was now a teenager. She had turned thirteen that week. On impulse I took a cameo necklace from my showcase and clasped it around her neck.

Tears spilled. With characteristic fervor she

vowed she would never take it off, *never,* she would wear it for*ever.*

Quizzing her as tactfully as I could, I learned only that Tina had four brothers and that her mother was an invalid. It wasn't so much that she was reluctant to talk about them as that our time together was short, and like any thirteen-year-old, she found herself to be an infinitely more fascinating topic of conversation.

In an attempt to wean her from the greasy french fries, the hamburgers and Cokes she bought at the farmhouse, I began bringing healthy lunches for her. She ate them to please me, but I doubt I was any more successful in converting her than I had been with Laurie at that age. Laurie's request for her thirteenth birthday celebration had been dinner at a local McDonald's with her best friend, Jenny Steele.

I haven't set foot in a fast-food factory since.

TINA STOPPED coming when the school year began in September. After wishing her father a good morning once or twice as I passed his table and getting a blank stare in return I said the hell with it.

After the season ended in late October, I never went back to Finney's Farm. I sold at Beacon the following winter and then my days of flea-marketing ended.

Once in a while, a hovering butterfly would remind me of Tina. In my mind she had remained a young and yearning thirteen forever.

# TWELVE

THE CASA GRECQUE restaurant is located in a shopping center near Lakeshore, a ten-minute drive from home. I've gone past it when I've needed supplies not available at the small, local hardware store where I prefer to buy, but I've never ventured inside.

There were several people waiting in the cool, wood-paneled foyer. Plants and a frosted glass partition screened it from the main dining room, where a hubbub of conversation competed with the strains of a Greek melody that sounded like "Never on Sunday" but wasn't.

The hostess, a striking white-haired woman dressed in a white silk shirt and a black skirt, gave me a practised smile. Her gaze dropped to the silver box in my hand and the smile widened and reached her eyes.

"The Spiridakis party?" she asked. "Are you Mrs. Wilde?"

"Yes."

"Upstairs." She pointed to my left. "The stairs are just around the corner, past the partition."

"Thank you."

"You're welcome." She touched my shoulder with light fingers. "Have fun," she said.

As I mounted the stairs I could feel them vibrating under my feet. A muffled roar, of music and laughter pulsated like the sea beyond the heavy oak on the top landing.

I took a deep breath, opened the door, and plunged in.

The room was large and well lit. And crowded. Tables were arranged around a dance floor, where a five-piece band on a raised platform thumped out a frantic version of "Billie Jean" above an undulating tide of dancers of all ages, from tots to fox-trotting old couples prudently circumnavigating their juniors.

"Catherine!"

Tina was suddenly beside me, slim and lovely in a pale mauve chiffon dress. She slipped her hand through my arm.

"Come on," she said. "Poppa and Alex are over here."

She piloted me to a corner of the room where the two men sat at a large, round table. They rose as we approached.

"You know Alex." Tina released my arm and moved to stand beside her fiancee. "You met him at Finney's."

"Of course. Hello, Alex."

"And you must remember my father," Tina said. "Poppa, you remember Catherine."

I extended my hand. "Mr. Spiridakis."

"Kostas." He took my hand in his. "Call me Kostas."

I had no more than a superficial memory of his face. Looking at him now it was obvious Tina had not inherited her beauty from her father.

His nose was prominent, high-bridged and broad, ending in a bulbous tip. Two deep grooves bracketed his rather thin, carved lips. His skin was coarse and sun-bronzed. His eyes, black as ripe olives, had lost the look of dark melacholy I remembered. They were sharp and humorous under thick, wild, gray brows. His grizzled hair had been pulled back tightly by a rubber band into a short ponytail.

He was thick-bodied and solid, about five-ten, Mike's height. He was dressed in a white-on-white shirt, open at the neck, sleeves rolled back above his elbows, separated from black pleated linen trousers by a paisley cummerbund. Four fat, dark cigars were lined up in his shirt pocket. There was a wide, plain gold wedding band on his left ring finger and a stainless steel watch on his wrist. His black tasseled loafers gleamed with polish.

Still holding my hand in his he gestured to the empty chair beside him.

"Please?"

Alex held the chair for me, sliding it expertly forward as I sat.

"Thank you." I looked up into his eyes, alive with good humor behind his small steel-rimmed glasses. "It's nice to see you again, Alex."

He smiled. "I'm glad you were able to come," he said. "Tina would have been very disappointed if you hadn't."

I turned to Tina and caught her signalling Alex with a frowning shake of her head. "Happy birthday," I said, and handed her the silver box.

Her eyes widened. "Oh," she said. "I didn't mean you to...you really shouldn't have."

"What's a birthday without gifts? Go ahead. Open it."

"Not yet." Kostas reached for the box. "Where are your manners, Christina? You haven't offered Mrs. Wilde so much as a cup of coffee."

Tina made a rueful face. "I'll be right back."

She hurried away. Three approving pairs of eyes followed her until she vanished through the moving wall of dancers.

"So." Kostas withdrew one of the cigars from his shirt pocket, bit off the tip, and dropped it in an ashtray. "Here we are. You were very kind to my Christina that summer, Mrs. Wilde."

"I was? It wasn't difficult. She was a bright, sensitive child. And she's grown up into a lovely young woman."

Kostas nodded, smiling. "Who looks like her mother, thank God," he said.

"Then her mother must be a beautiful woman."

"She was." He struck a kitchen match with his thumbnail and applied the flame to his cigar. He drew on it until the tip glowed, then took the cigar from his lips and said, "She died three years ago."

"Oh. I'm sorry."

Kostas blew out a cloud of fragrant smoke and watched it disperse. "Thank you," he said simply.

Tina reappeared a moment later with a cup and saucer in her hand, accompanied by two young women, one with a pitcher of cream, the other carrying a sugar bowl.

Tina set the cup filled with coffee in front of me. "I'd like you to meet my sisters-in-law. Julia and Alice, this is my friend Catherine Wilde."

Julia was cream, plump and pretty, the elder of the two; Alice was sugar, a young woman with large glasses and long blond hair. Both welcomed me with gracious smiles, both hurried away when Kostas interrupted their chatter.

"Birthday cake," he demanded. "Maybe Mrs. Wilde would like a slice of birthday cake."

"Trish and Debbie are bringing the cake," Tina said.

"I'll bet they are," Alex said, grinning up at Tina. She scowled at him and smacked the back of his head. Laughing, he caught her hand and kissed it.

"That's my girl," he chortled.

Trish and Debbie and the cake arrived. Tina introduced them. Two more sisters-in-law with warm greetings, charming smiles, and a hasty departure.

"Well." Tina dropped into the chair between her

father and Alex and expelled a deep breath. "You happy now, Poppa? Can I open my gift?"

Kostas waved his cigar magnanimously.

Tina opened the silver box. She lifted the butterfly from its nest of tissue paper. The faceted crystal captured the light and glittered with white fire.

"It's your sun-struck butterfly," I explained.

Tina looked at me, starry-eyed.

"You remembered," she breathed. "You *remembered*. Thank you, Catherine. It's beautiful. I'll keep it forever."

"What is this, sun-struck." Kostas frowned. "What kind of butterfly is a sun-struck?"

Before Tina or I could speak, a middle-aged man with a shock of white hair leaned into the table.

"Kostas!" he shouted above the sudden blare of the music winding up to a noisy finale. "Where are the boys? I wanted to talk to them about the fund-raising banquet!"

Kostas raised both palms and held them up until the music ended with a final crash. He removed the cigar from his lips.

"Demetrios won't come up until he closes the restaurant downstairs," he said. "Petros, Ari, and Stavros had a cocktail party catering." He glanced down at his watch. "It should be over by now. They'll be here soon."

"Would you tell Petros I'd like a few minutes?"

Kostas gestured with his head. "Tell him yourself."

The crush of dancers had dispersed, leaving the floor around the bandstand empty. Three men, wearing identical white blazers and black trousers, strode purposefully toward us, the tallest a pace ahead.

There was no mistaking who they were. The leader was a youthful Kostas, with coal black hair, expertly shaped to a large head. The eyes, the nose, the deep grooves carved from nostrils to chin, the broad, muscular build, all were Kostas.

A step behind was a strikingly handsome male edition of Tina. The third man had the nose but not the chunky body. He was thin, almost to the point of delicacy, and walked with a perceptible limp.

The white-haired man intercepted them.

"Hey, Petros," he addressed the tallest of the three, "we've got to get together. Time's flying."

"Later, Theo, okay? I'll come find you."

"Sure. But don't forget me."

"I won't."

Petros shrugged out of the white blazer and draped it over the back of the chair opposite me. He yanked at his black bow tie, leaving the ends hanging, unbuttoned the collar of his white shirt, and dropped himself into the chair facing Kostas.

"Okay, Pop," he said. "Bottom-line time. We signed the lease for the new restaurant today. When are you going to give up the flea-market shit and—" He stopped at a frown from his father. "Sorry, Pop. When will you be ready to take over this place?"

Kostas shook his head. "Not yet," he said mildly.

"Okay. When?"

"I don't know. Not yet."

"Look, Pop. Demetrios goes to the new setup. Ari and Stavros don't have it, you know that. I'm up to my eyeballs with the catering business. We'll have to hire some stranger to manage this place."

"Then maybe that's what you'd better do."

The two men locked eyes and wills in a silent, private battle. The handsome son had vanished from the field. The slim, lame son had fixed his gaze on some far horizon.

Seconds ticked by, then Petros grunted and turned to Tina and Alex.

"You guys better plan to elope," he said, "because your wedding money is going to go into some stranger's pocket."

Kostas stiffened. "I will pay for my daughter's wedding," he said in an ominously quiet voice.

"With what, Pop?" Petros snapped. "With the crap you lug around in that beat-up old truck of yours?"

"I will have the money," Kostas said.

"Sure you will. Tell me exactly how you—"

"Enough!" The word cut like a knife. Kostas fixed his son with coal black eyes.

"Remember, please," he said coldly. "I am your father. I am not some *vlaka* you can bully. I have told you. I will have the money. Christina will have her wedding."

Petros's eyes narrowed, but he backed off. Shrugging, he raised his hands and said, "All right, Poppa. All right."

He dropped his hands as the band started up a slow, stately melody. He looked at his father, a rueful smile on his craggy face.

Kostas grinned back. "They're playing our song," he said and rose to his feet. "Come on, boys."

They left us, the three Spiridakis men and Alex, and walked out onto the dance floor. Tina moved into the chair beside me and we watched others join them in the measured dance I've often seen in bits and pieces on the screen, never in life.

As the dance proceeded I found my eyes following Kostas. He moved with a serene, fluid dignity, every part of him wed to the measured beat of the ancient music. Watching him I felt that rare and joyous sense of wonder that floods like sunrise when perfection takes human form, and I remembered a bowling tournament Mike insisted I attend with him.

Sports bore me, any sport. I sat sulking until the performance of one of the bowlers captured my attention. His play was pure grace, and I forgot I was watching a silly game. Mike's comment had been, *"Of course. The man's a champion."*

And now, Kostas.

"Your father is a beautiful dancer," I said to Tina. I was surprised to find I had been holding my breath.

"My father is a beautiful man," Tina said. She

leaned forward to look into my face. "Do you like him?"

"I don't really…"

The eager expression in Tina's eyes stopped me. I could almost hear the clicking as all the little round balls dropped into all their little round holes.

The urgent invitation, made impossible to refuse. Four sisters-in-law to deliver one cup of coffee and one piece of cake? Alex's amusement. The warning scowl, the glancing slap on the back of his head and his laughing response.

Tina was matchmaking.

"Tina," I said, "I've already got a fella."

Her cheeks flushed scarlet. Then she giggled.

"Damn," she said. "Alex told me I can't do subtle." She glanced away at the sound of her name. "They want us to come," she said.

Kostas and Alex were waving for us to join them.

"Are you kidding?" I protested. "I can't do that stuff."

"Sure you can."

She took me firmly by the hand and hauled me onto the floor, where for two minutes I made a fool of myself trying to do something that wasn't as easy as it looked. I was relieved when the band took a two-beat pause and slid into a waltz. Kostas touched my shoulder.

"May I have this dance?" he said.

"Are you sure you want to? I don't think my feet are connected to my brain today."

"Trust me."

With a deferential foot of space between us, he placed his right hand in the small of my back and guided me smoothly and expertly into the flow of dancers.

"I'm sorry for the family scene," he apologized. "Petros gets impatient when things don't go his way, but there was no excuse for him being rude in front of a stranger."

"He probably finds it hard to understand why you would prefer flea-marketing."

"Do you? Do you understand?"

I started to make a noncommittal reply, but the expression in Kostas's dark eyes demanded an honest answer.

"No, I don't."

"It's very simple," Kostas said. "I'm having fun."

"*Fun?* Flea-marketing?"

Kostas smiled. He waltzed me to the perimeter of the dance floor, farthest from the band, where it was quieter.

"My parents came to this country from Greece," he said, "and opened a mom-and-pop corner grocery store. Except it wasn't just Mama and Papa. It was the whole family. I put stickers on cans when I was four. I graduated from floor sweeper to delivery boy to clerk. Every day after school, every weekend. We all worked. And always, pounded into our heads, *the customer is God*. Then one day the supermarkets came and God took his business to the A and P.''

I couldn't help laughing. Charlton Heston in flowing robes and beard, pushing a grocery cart. Kostas smiled.

"So I became a waiter," he continued. "And fell in love with the boss's daughter, and only the saints know why, but she loved me back. My beautiful Marina. And we were married and God gave us four sons and Christina. And when Marina's parents went back to Greece, the restaurant was ours, and we all worked, except Stavros, who was sickly, and Christina, who was a child. And like it was in the grocery store of my parents, the customer was God.''

The music stopped and Kostas's hand fell away from my back. He made no move to leave the dance floor. He looked into my face, his eyes blackly amused.

"Please excuse the expression," he said, "but one day I realized most of my life I've spent kissing the public's ass.''

The band suddenly struck up the all-too-familiar opening chords of "Achy Breaky Heart." Kostas and I exchanged horrified glances and he hustled me back to the round table.

"So you gave up the restaurant because you were tired of catering to the public?" I prompted.

Kostas shook his head. "It wasn't that easy. Do you know what *fascio-scapular-humeral* is?"

"No.''

"It's a disease where the muscle nerve cells die. It mostly hits people over forty. They get weaker and weaker until the muscles won't work anymore. They live maybe ten years after. There's no cure."

"That's awful."

"It's a curse from God. It got Marina. When she couldn't walk or even raise her hand to feed herself anymore, I closed the restaurant and sold the building and stayed with her until there was nothing left."

"Kostas, I'm so sorry."

Kostas nodded. "Yes," he said. He was silent a moment.

"When Marina died," he continued, "I gave the boys the money that was left and they opened this restaurant. I had sold off all the old restaurant furniture and equipment at Finney's—that's when Christina met you—and I started picking up junk and selling at a couple of other markets." He shrugged. "And now I do the flea markets."

"And you're having fun?"

Kostas's face split in a wide and beautiful grin.

"Like my boys used to say, I'm having a ball," he said. "For the first time in my life the customer isn't God. For the first time in my life I don't have to be nice and polite even when it's killing me. If I don't like somebody's face I can tell them *ade gamisou malaka*."

"Does that mean what I think it means?"

Kostas laughed. "Probably. Loosely translated, if

you pardon the expression, it means fuck off, buster.''

I hooted. I was accustomed to Mike's blue language and no longer heard the words, but there was a primness in Kostas that made the trite obscenity somehow new and funny. Kostas simply smiled.

"Would you like something to drink?" he said. "Maybe a liqueur? A glass of wine?"

"Thank you, no." I hesitated. "What I would really like, without being rude, is to go home. I was up very early, and it's been a long day. Would that offend you? Do you think Tina would mind?"

"Of course not." He rose to his feet. "I'll walk you to your car."

"Would you make my excuses to Tina?" I indicated the surge of line dancers. "I'll never find her in there."

"Of course."

We skirted the dance floor and descended the stairs to the foyer below. The white-haired woman gave us a smile and a wave as we went out in the warm summer night.

Above the horizon the moon hung like a misty pink gumdrop in the dusky bowl of the sky. The mall lights dimmed the stars. We stood a moment and watched the night-flying moths in their futile assaults on the incandescent globes. Then Kostas cupped my elbow with his palm and walked me to my car.

I unlocked the door and extended my hand.

"It was nice meeting you again, Kostas. I'll probably see you at Finney's this Friday."

He shook his head. "Not this week. I have some business to clear up. Next Friday."

"Next week, then. Good night."

"Good night, Catherine."

He waved as I started the engine, then turned and walked back into the Casa Grecque.

# THIRTEEN

WHEN I ARRIVED at Finney's early Friday morning, Old Sam was in place and all set up. He waved me out of the van, parked it expertly and helped me unload.

An hour later, setting up completed, I poured two mugs of thermos coffee, one for Old Sam, one for myself.

"No muffin?" he asked.

"Bagel and cream cheese."

I handed him the foil-wrapped bagel and the coffee mug. He took them, smiling.

"Ah, Catherine," he said, in that Bogey lisp, "you are a woman of rare taste and discrimination."

"You bet I am."

With nothing new on display, my tables were ignored by the scavenging dealers and I was able to sit back and enjoy my second breakfast.

The morning air was cool and sweet, uncontaminated by stale grease odors, which had not yet escaped the cinderblock kitchen of the old farmhouse, and "Achy Breaky Heart" had been muted to an inoffensive level by the Cooley vigilantes. After a minor rush, Old Sam was dickering good-naturedly with Lionel over a set of English horse brasses.

It was almost nine before I made my first sale. But it was worth waiting for.

A slender woman with a sculpted cap of snow white hair who had been casually browsing along my table suddenly shrieked *"Dick Whittington!"* and lunged for the Royal Doulton Toby jug.

"How much are you asking for this?" Her voice was high-pitched, her accent veddy British. Her blue eyes sparkled with excitement.

"It's marked." I indicated the sticker on the handle. "Two hundred dollars."

"Oh. Of course. I beg your pardon." She turned the jug in her hands. "It isn't cracked or chipped is it?"

"I don't think so. It would be marked 'as is.' But check it, please. People at flea markets tend not to handle things as carefully as they should."

"Of course." She withdrew a pair of glasses from her bag, propped them on her nose, and examined the jug minutely. Satisfied, she removed the glasses and smiled at me.

"It's perfect," she pronounced. "I'll take it. Do you know how long I've been searching for Dick Whittington? Ages, my dear. They're a fortune in England. At least twice what you are asking. I'm so delighted. I'm absolutely thrilled!"

I reached for the jug. "I'm so glad."

"Hey, lady. What's your best price on this?"

I glanced down at the cast-iron frying pan thrust under my nose. It was marked six-fifty.

"Six dollars," I said and moved away to get a bag.

I brought the Toby jug back to the English woman, safely wrapped, and she paid me.

"I only hope I can carry it on the plane home without breaking it," she worried.

"Popcorn," I told her. "Pack it in popcorn."

"Popcorn! What a marvelous idea. I will. Thank you."

"Thank you. And have a good flight home."

I gave her my widest smile and watched her saunter away, cradling her purchase in her arms.

"Hey, lady. This here is a used frying pan. It ain't worth six bucks. Come on. You can do better than six bucks."

I glared at the frying pan, then up a hairy arm into Mike's grinning face.

"Gotcha," he said.

Snatching the pan from his hand, I set it down on the table with a thump and said, "Get lost, mister,"

Mike chortled. He limped around to the rear of my setup and sidled through the narrow space between the van and the tables. By the time he came up behind me there were six people demanding attention.

"Is it always this busy?" he asked, watching me drop a slightly scratched red Tonka truck into a plastic bag and hand it to a small male child who was the spitting image of his obese father.

"It's July." I gave the boy the change and received a scowl from his daddy. "Tourists. People on vacation. The kids are out of school. The cottage people are up for the summer. Finney's is something to do on a Friday, and where else can the whole fandamily spend the day without buying tickets?"

A woman waved a rhinestone-studded dog collar at me and I went to serve her.

After three sales in quick succession suddenly there were no more customers. It was close to noon, lunchtime. I went back to where Mike sat, his eyes on Old Sam.

"Mike? I want to take a fast run around and see if I can find a piece of old silk for Charlie's sewing table. Do you think you can handle this for about a half hour?"

"Sure." Mike tilted his head in Old Sam's direction. "Any more drug deals this morning?" he asked softly.

"Not that I saw."

"You go ahead. I'll keep an eye open."

"The book box is right there, on the corner of Old Sam's table," I said under my breath.

"Okay. I'll watch it."

I went off, unconsciously matching my stride to the line-dance beat of "Achy Breaky Heart," marching up one lane and down the next, stopping only to rummage through piles of old clothing and linens.

I found a pair of softly faded cotton damask drapes and bought them as backup. At another ven-

dor's table I saw an ancient mink coat lined with
pale silk damask, but I could easily have pushed a
finger through the brittle fabric, so I passed on it.
Too bad.

Hurrying back, I was stopped dead in my tracks,
as abruptly as if I had run into a brick wall. I looked
around, frowning. What had I seen? What had my
eye picked up?

Then I saw it.

Two years ago, I restored a plant stand for Charlie
and Rafe, stripping away the ugly olive green paint
somebody attempting to be, as Rafe put it, *'God help
us, creative'*, had used to turn a genuine antique into
a phony antique.

Under the paint I had found beautiful old mahog-
any. The carved water lilies on the tall, slender legs
had proved to be bronze, not wood at all.

That plant stand was the first—and also the last—
Louis Majorelle I've ever seen. And I was looking
at it now.

I went to it, not believing my eyes. How had the
crack-of-dawn dealers missed it? The price on the
sticker was forty-five dollars. I touched the smooth
finish, my mind in turmoil. It was either my Majorelle—and that simply was not possible—or a very,
very clever imitation.

"Can I help you?"

I started guiltily. Forty-five dollars was a steal for
the plant stand, genuine Majorelle or not. And I intended to steal it. I looked up into the vendor's face.

It was Brady, Old Sam's current bête noire. He stood almost into my space, tall and slightly stoop-shouldered, his arms and hands dangling loosely.

"I was looking at this plant stand."

He nodded, waiting.

"I think I'll take it," I said, and added offhand-edly, "Where does it come from?"

"I'm sorry. I don't know." He had a low, pleas-ant voice. "I picked it up at an auction."

I gave him the forty-five dollars. He accepted it with a smile, and I understood why Rena had been so defensive when she had spoken of him. The smile transformed his face from a scruffy-bearded, leftover hippy to that of a delighted boy.

It was an ingenuous, infectious smile, and I smiled back at him as automatically as I imagine most people would—with the possible exception of Old Sam.

"Young man!" A sharp voice cut between us. "We've been waiting here very patiently. Now, do you intend to serve us or not?"

"Excuse me." Brady dipped his head and turned to them. I picked up the plant stand and hustled back to my tables.

Mike was dickering with a gray-haired man over a handful of paperback books, looking as though he was thoroughly enjoying himself. I put the plant stand inside the van and went to serve a sudden surge of customers.

"That was fun," Mike said when the rush was

over. He handed me a fistful of small bills and change. "Eighteen bucks. Ten for books, five for a glass bowl, and three for a jar full of buttons. Why the hell would anybody buy a jar full of buttons?"

"Old buttons are collectible. They're probably hoping they'll find a couple of good ones in the jar."

"Will they?"

"I doubt it. Not at three dollars for the lot."

"Are old banged-up tin bread boxes collectible?"

"What do you mean?"

"Sam sold a rusty bread box to three very well-dressed Oriental dudes who paid him with a folded wad of bills that had to be an inch thick. He didn't count the money, just shoved it into his pocket. And he didn't give them change."

Mike frowned past me at Old Sam. "I still think I know the guy from somewhere. I've met him. I'm positive."

"Did you get a chance to talk to him?"

"No. That jerk's been bending his ear since you left."

I glanced across to where Old Sam stood, his arms folded across his chest, his head lowered, listening.

"The jerk is Shifty George."

"That's Shifty George?" Mike raised his eyebrows. "He doesn't look so bad."

Viewed through Mike's eyes, I suppose he didn't. He's square and solid, with powerful arms and shoulders and big hands. His legs are short for his torso. Were they in proportion, he'd be a tall man.

His face is broad, a Slav face, with small, almost colorless eyes.

He combs his dun-colored hair straight back, the way I remember my father did in the thirties. Somehow, that hairstyle and the florid manners, natural or adopted, mark him as vaguely Continental, an illusion enhanced by his manner of dress. He favors white shirts with the sleeves folded precisely back. Always a tie. Pressed chinos or gray flannels with a knife edge. And thin-soled, expensive shoes.

"There was a woman named Terry," I told Mike, "who set up one summer at Beacon. She was a flight attendant, I don't remember which airline, and she was moonlighting to pay off her charge cards. She was attractive, a little bit wacky, but very funny and a genuinely nice person."

Shifty George looked up at that moment and caught me watching him. He bowed slightly from the waist, raised his hand palm up, the way the pope does it, and smiled the smile that makes my flesh crawl, all teeth and cold, watchful eyes.

"George hit on her from day one. Terry couldn't stand him. Short of getting downright nasty, she let him know every which way she could that she didn't appreciate the off-color remarks, and that she didn't like being groped."

A customer demanded Old Sam's attention. He left George standing and went to serve her. Shifty George glared after him, then turned and walked away, his face flushed.

"One Sunday," I continued, "Terry and I were chatting when George came along. He grabbed her by the shoulders and he said, 'Kiss me, it's my birthday, ha-ha.' Terry looked him dead in the eye and said, 'George, I'd rather kiss the pink butt on a bare-assed baboon.' No anger. Totally deadpan."

Mike grinned. "Jesus," he said.

"Uhuh," I agreed. "The thing is, except for me, nobody heard her say it. It wasn't said loud enough for anyone else to hear. If George was humiliated—which I doubt, you can't insult the man—it was a very limited humiliation. But when Terry went to load at the end of the day, all four tires on her car had been slashed. She never came back."

"You sure George did it?"

"Who else? Everybody liked Terry."

BY TWO O'CLOCK we were into a full-blown hot and humid July day. Mike and I sat on camp chairs fanning ourselves and watching the flushed and sweating world flow listlessly past.

"What's the matter with these people?" Mike said. "You can drop dead on a day like this. Why don't they go home?"

"Who knows?" I fanned the heavy air. "Who cares?"

"Who's that?"

Striding toward us, cutting through the aimless drifters in her path, was a young woman in a yellow sundress and a floppy straw hat. Huge sunglasses hid half her face. She came to a halt at Old Sam's table, where Old Sam bent rearranging the contents of his jewelry case. She tapped the top of his head with a rigid forefinger.

Old Sam snapped upright. The flash of anger on his face was instantly replaced by a delighted smile.

"Sandy! What are you doing here?"

There was no answering smile on the mouth beneath those big dark sunglasses.

"Where have you been?" the woman demanded.

Without waiting for an answer, she turned and marched up the narrow lane alongside his tables.

"Where have you been all week?" she asked again, squeezing past the corner of Old Sam's van and advancing on him. "I've called you every day. No answer."

"I'm sorry, honey," he began.

"Don't honey me." She removed the glasses and glared at him. "I even went by your place on Wednesday after work. You know what I thought? I thought you were dead. I expected to find you stretched out on the floor. Or in the bathtub. Or in bed. Dead."

"Sorry to disappoint you." Old Sam offered a smile.

The anger melted from the slim figure. Her shoulders dropped. She sighed and shook her head at him.

"Darn it, Daddy," she said plaintively. "You could have called. You could have called me."

"I know. I've been doing a lot of running around.

But I should have called. I'm sorry, honey." Old Sam touched her cheek gently. "It won't happen again. I promise. So, what are you doing here? Why aren't you at work?"

"Where else was I going to look? I took the day off. I figured this is where you'd have to be today—if you were still alive."

With a sweep of her hand she took in the entire flea market. Her eye fell on Mike and me, rapt as spectators at a performance.

"Where's Rena?" she asked.

"Off sick," Sam said. "Catherine's filling in for her. Catherine? Mike? This is my daughter Sandy."

"How do you do," she said, smiling at us. It was Old Sam's smile, and her eyes, large and thickly lashed, were the same smoke gray as her father's.

Mike rose from the camp chair. "Would you like to sit down, Sandy?"

"No, no. Thank you. I'm not staying. While I'm here, I think I'll go pick up some fresh veggies." She turned to Old Sam. "How about supper tonight?"

"Not tonight. Sorry, Sandy, I can't tonight. I had a call from a woman selling off her mother's estate up at Lake Echo, and I'm going there directly from here. Can we make it tomorrow night?"

Sandy nodded. "Fine. I'll pick up the makings on the way and cook at your place. But don't you dare forget and stand me up, Daddy. *Remember*. Tomorrow."

"Tomorrow it is." Sam raised his eyebrows. "Saturday night? You're not seeing old jerk-face?"

Sandy sighed with the exaggerated patience children of any age reserve for their parents. "No, Daddy, I am not seeing old jerk-face. Paul and I broke up last week."

"Good. I never liked him."

"I know. And he did too." She kissed his cheek, waved to Mike and me. "Nice meeting you two," she said, and was gone.

"Nice girl," Mike observed when she could no longer be seen.

Old Sam nodded. "Yes. I got lucky, for once."

MIKE HELPED ME pack and load the van. When we were finished he wiped his streaming face with the wet towel I bring on hot days for just that purpose.

"I take back what I said before," he groaned. "This isn't fun. It's pig labor. Rena does this every week?"

"Every week. All year round. Winter and summer."

"Jesus. It'd be like packing a house for a move, over and over. How many houses do you figure she does in a year?"

"Who counts? You don't think about it. You just do it."

"Hell of a way to make a buck." He handed me the towel. "My car's in the parking lot. Want to meet somewhere on the way and grab a bite to eat?"

"Thanks, Mike. Let's not. All I want to do is to get home, get out of these clothes and under a cold shower."

"Yeah. Okay. I'll call you tomorrow." He walked away, waving to Old Sam as he passed.

I climbed into the van, started it up, and set the air conditioner on high, rolling down the window to wave good-bye to Old Sam.

"So long, Catherine," he called. "See you Sunday."

I never saw Old Sam again.

# FOURTEEN

THE MAJORELLE PLANT STAND must have been on my mind. I dreamed I was stripping it again. The more paint I scraped away, the smaller it became until it disappeared entirely, leaving me with only a foul-smelling green puddle.

In the morning I brought the stand from the van and set it in the kitchen. I stared at it while I ate breakfast.

Had Majorelle produced dozens of identical plant stands, or only the one? Was this the one? Was it a copy? Was this the plant stand I had worked on? And what difference did it make, anyway? What did it matter?

It mattered. I don't leave a mark on any of the pieces I restore, but I like to think I would recognize my own work. I knew I wouldn't be able to leave it alone until I had an answer, and the only way to get an answer was to show the stand to Charlie and Rafe.

To justify the drive into town on a muggy July Saturday, I decided to stop in at the Salvation Army depot, with the hope of finding a piece of silk damask large enough and old enough to replace the workbag on the Victorian sewing table.

After an hour of rummaging in the Sally Ann's airless basement room, the stench of ancient sweat, cheap perfume, and moth balls was too much for me. Faintly nauseous and dripping perspiration, I fled, empty-handed, and drove across town to the lane behind Canterbury House Antiques.

Clutching the plant stand, I banged a fist on the shop's metal-faced delivery room door. After what seemed forever, the door opened narrowly and Charlie glared out. When he realized who it was, he swung the door wide.

"Cat? What the hell...?"

I walked past him and set the planter upright on the floor. "This," I said. "Do you recognize it?"

He eyed the stand. "It looks familiar. Am I supposed to recognize it?"

"Two years ago I stripped a Louis Majorelle plant stand for you guys. Olive green paint. Remember? Is this it?"

Charlie picked up the stand, turned it upside down and looked at the underside, peering closely at the top of one of the legs.

"It's ours." He raised his head. "Where'd you get it?"

"How do you know it's yours?"

"Here." Charlie pointed to a three-quarter circle, no larger than a dime. Inside the arc were the initials *C.H.* "Canterbury House," Charlie explained. "We burn it into every piece of furniture that goes through our hands. Started doing it after somebody tried to palm off a fake, claiming they'd bought it from us.''

He set the planter down. ''Where'd you get it?''

''Finney's. Yesterday. I paid forty-five dollars for it.''

''What!'' Charlie roared.

''I bought it from a vendor at—''

''I heard you! I just don't believe it.'' Charlie snatched up the planter. ''Come on, Cat.''

I followed him into the shop, where Rafe was putting porcelain figurines into a glass-fronted cabinet.

''They bought the Lenci head,'' he told Charlie.

''Never mind the Lenci head.'' Charlie slammed the planter on the floor in front of Rafe. ''Recognize this?''

Rafe merely glanced at the stand. ''The Majorelle,'' he said, and looked at me. ''You stripped it, Cat. Remember?''

''Who did we sell it to?'' Charlie demanded before I could reply.

''Léli Steinhauer.'' Rafe frowned. ''Charlie, what—''

Charlie held up a hand. ''How much were we asking for it?''

''Twenty-five hundred.'' Rafe eyed me, then Charlie. ''You mind telling me...''

Charlie flipped his palm at me. ''Tell him, Cat.''

''I bought it from a vendor at Finney's yesterday. I paid him forty-five dollars for it.''

Rafe's eyes narrowed. "By any remote chance, did you ask him where he got it?"

I nodded. "He said he picked it up at auction."

"Not possible," Rafe stated quietly. "We're at every auction in town. We'd have spotted it."

"Maybe out of town," I suggested.

"Absolutely out of the question," Charlie said. "Léli would never place anything out for auction without giving us first refusal."

Charlie and Rafe looked at one another.

"Something's wrong here, Charlie," Rafe said. "When did we last see Léli?"

"A couple of months? No, I'm wrong. It was just before Easter. She brought us a bowl of narcissus for the shop."

"Easter?" Rafe frowned. "I didn't think it was that long ago. I think we should call her."

Charlie nodded. He turned away and headed for the rear of the shop, where a state-of-the art telephone setup sat incongruously on a superb mid-Georgian partners desk. Rafe and I trailed behind him.

"Tempus fugits too fast," Charlie muttered, riffling the pages of a gilt-edged, morocco-bound address book.

"Don't mention the Majorelle," Rafe cautioned.

Casting a withering glance at him, Charlie tapped out the numbers and waited. His face brightened.

"Dr. Steinhauer? Léli? It's Charlie. Charles Harwood." He listened for a moment, then said, "I know. It's been a while. How are you?"

He frowned. After a moment he perched on the corner of the desk, one leg swinging.

"Léli," he said, "you should have called us. We'd have come to visit." He listened, nodding. "Why not today? Why not now?" he asked, and then stood up. "Good. See you in a half hour or so."

He replaced the receiver, pulling at his lower lip.

"She fell and broke her hip two months ago." Charlie turned to me. "Cat? Gordon has the van out. Would you mind driving me? It's not far. The new town house complex overlooking the river. Gleneagles Court."

"I don't mind. I'll drive you there."

"How does she sound, Charlie?" Rafe asked.

"Subdued. Apparently the bone isn't knitting well, and she's stuck in her bed."

"Stop at a florist on the way. She likes yellow roses."

"I know she does. I'll pick up a dozen."

THE FIRST FLORIST SHOP had no yellow roses, nor the second. After some ten minutes Charlie emerged from the third with a long, gray box.

"Yellow roses?" I asked, starting the car.

"Yellow roses. Three florists, for Christ's sake. Anybody else and I'd have said the hell with it."

"She must be pretty special. Who is she?"

Charlie settled himself into the bucket seat with the box on his knees, and as I threaded my way through midtown traffic, he told me about Léli Steinhauer.

# FIFTEEN

...WE MET Léli's husband first.

We'd only been open a couple of months when he came into the shop. Skinny, tall, stoop-shouldered. We figured he was somewhere in his sixties.

He wandered around, picking up this, picking up that. Mostly he looked at us. We were used to it by then, people staring. It didn't bother us. What bothered us was he left without buying. Those early days were a bugger. We weren't sure we'd survive.

He came back a week later and did his wandering act again.

In the meanwhile, we'd picked up this sterling thing. Rafe hadn't done any research yet, and we hadn't the foggiest what it was. It was about nine inches tall, a filigree box on a stem rising from a solid base. There was a steeple on the box with a flag finial. Hallmarked, with some Hebrew writing around the box.

The old boy pounced on it.

That's how we met Aaron. He introduced himself.

He was Dr. Aaron Steinhauer. He was a plastic surgeon, and he collected Judaica, which is what our sterling thing was. A Judaica piece.

He told us it was a spice box, English origin, not all that old, and worth the hundred-and-fifty-dollar price we had slapped on it. He bought it, asked us to call if we ran across anything in the way of Judaica, and left. Hell, up till then we hadn't even known there were such things as Judaica collectibles.

He was back a few days later with an absolutely stunning woman. Do you remember Ava Gardner in her fifties? And Simone Signoret? Those marvelous faces, with all the wear and tear on them and still beautiful? That was Léli.

He introduced us. His wife, Dr. Lélia Steinhauer. Back then, she was head of pediatrics at Jewish General. And she collected miniatures. Almost anything, she told us, as long as it's small. And beautiful. And perfect.

They began dropping by regularly. Usually late in the day, sometimes on a Saturday.

We became...I guess you could say we became friends, although we never saw them outside the shop. They both had demanding careers, and Rafe and I were putting in seven days a week, trying to stay afloat.

In the beginning they'd browse, chat a little, and buy or not buy. They began bringing a bottle of wine when they came late in the day, and we'd sip and talk, and after a couple of years we got to know one another pretty well.

They were DPs. Remember in the late forties and

early fifties, after the war ended? All the displaced persons who came to this country?

Aaron and Léli met in one of the DP camps set up by the Allies after the war. Both had lost their families. Their only child, a boy they named Noah after Aaron's father, was born in that camp.

Twenty-two years later Noah died in Vietnam.

"SHIT." Charlie leaned forward against the seat belt and glared out the windshield. "I wasn't paying attention. We've missed the goddam exit. We'll have to take the next one and backtrack. Dammit. I'm really sorry, Cat."

"Hey, Charlie, It's no big deal. Relax."

He did. And took up where he had left off...

...BY THE END OF the fourth year we knew we were going to make it. The shop was on solid ground, and we were doing four antique shows a year. The big ones.

We were slowly gaining access to estates, but we were still running like sons of bitches—which is probably why we weren't aware of how long it had been since we'd seen Aaron and Léli. Time flies when every day is a scramble.

Then we picked up an Esther holder and scroll we knew Aaron would like and we realized we hadn't seen them for a month or more. Actually, when we stopped to think about it, it was closer to six months.

I never liked calling them at the hospital, it seemed such an intrusion, so we waited until evening.

Léli answered the phone. I think I made some asinine remark, typical motormouth me. I absolutely do not remember what I said, but it had to have been pretty stupid because there was no reaction at the other end of the line.

So I told Léli what we had and asked her if she thought Aaron might be interested. She thanked me and said she'd come down to the shop in the morning. She sounded distant, not like herself at all.

I remember telling Rafe something was wrong.

Both Rafe and I were busy attending to customers when we saw her come in. I asked her if she would mind waiting, I wouldn't be long. She didn't say anything. She didn't smile. She just nodded. Not like Léli at all.

She drifted, not really looking at anything, until we were free. When we got together at the rear of the shop, she told us bluntly that Aaron had cancer. That Aaron was dying.

"He has two months, maybe three," she said. "I'll be bringing him home this weekend. He doesn't want to die among strangers. He asked me to say good-bye for him."

She looked at me, at Rafe, at our shocked faces.

"Please understand," she said. "He doesn't want you to see him the way he is now."

That rigid control of hers almost cracked. She

looked away. We could see her fighting for composure.

Rafe slipped out and came back with a small package.

"Give this to Aaron for his collection," he said. "Tell him we miss him. Tell him we will always miss him."

That's when she broke down. Rafe shoved the package at me and took her in his arms. She cried without a sound, which still amazes me. Every other woman I've known bawls.

Rafe held her until she stopped shaking. He let his arms drop and she stepped away from him, swiping at her nose with the back of her hand, the way a kid does.

"I'm sorry," she said, as though she had done something to be ashamed of. She took the package from me and held it tightly in her arms. "Thank you for this, both of you. Aaron will be pleased."

We walked with her to the shop entrance.

"If you need anything, *anything,* you call," Rafe said.

"If I need anything, I will."

She gave us the saddest smile I've ever seen and left us standing in the doorway. We watched her get into her car and drive away. I didn't think she'd call. Neither did Rafe.

But she did.

She called two months later, and we went to

Aaron's funeral. It was a nondenominational service, no flowers. Neither Aaron nor Léli believed in any God any longer, and they asked everybody to donate to cancer research instead of sending flowers.

At the grave, Léli detached herself from a group of people who looked to be exactly what they probably were, hospital colleagues of hers and of Aaron's. She came over to where we stood.

She had lost a lot of weight but she was still Léli, head high and so damn heartbreakingly beautiful in her black dress.

"Thank you for coming," she said. "Aaron asked me to be sure to thank you for the Esther scroll. He asked me to tell you it's a thing of beauty and he'll pay you for it the next time around."

She looked back at the group clustered around the open grave. They were all watching us.

"I'd better go back," she said. "Thank you, Charlie. Thank you, Rafe." She kissed my cheek, then Rafe's. "I'll call you," she said.

"THERE'S OUR EXIT, Cat," Charlie said.

I slowed for the long exit-ramp curve.

"You'll have to tell me where to go from here," I said. "I'm lost in this neck of the woods."

"Just ahead. On the left there. The iron gates. That's Gleneagles Court."

# SIXTEEN

THE ELABORATE wrought-iron gates stood open and served no practical purpose whatsoever. They were set into brick pillars topped with antiqued lanterns on either side of the road into the complex. No fence, no wall. So why bother with gates?

"Cheaper than a drawbridge," Charlie said. "And the city probably wouldn't let them dig a moat."

We drove past the gate and down the winding road, shaded by tall trees and flanked by espaliered stone walls. Large brass signs etched with names like Coventry Place and Maidstone Lane and Nottingham Corner, announced the side streets.

"Whatever happened to just plain 'street'?" I asked.

"Don't be crass," Charlie said. "No cachet in street."

"What are we looking for?"

"Plymouth Way. Léli's on Plymouth Way."

"Cute. Where is it?"

"God knows. Keep going. It's in here somewhere."

I drove slowly. The road was a series of S-curves,

no doubt laid out to discourage speeding. On the tail of the final S we found ourselves back at the gates.

"What the hell?" Charlie grunted. "We missed it."

I pointed. "Is there a map on that board?"

"Hold on." Charlie got out of the car, crossed the road, and peered at an iron-framed board mounted on a stone wall just inside the gates. He came trotting back.

"Plymouth Way is off Maidstone Lane," he said. "Christ, I'd hate to be the mailman in this place."

Maidstone wasn't a lane and Plymouth wasn't a way. They were pockets of town houses. Maidstone had six, cottage-style, with gray cedar-shake roofs suggestive of thatch, Plymouth had five, vaguely Tudor. The houses had been erected at angles to one another, in a pattern designed to provide maximum privacy on minimum footage. Open carports connected them.

We crawled through Maidstone into Plymouth.

"Which house is Léli's?"

Charlie pointed. "The one with the green door."

"That's not green." I came to a stop in front of the center house. "It's turquoise."

"Green, turquoise, whatever." Charlie clambered out of the car, florist box under his arm. He bent and raised an eyebrow at me through the car window. "Well?" he said. "Come on."

"I'll wait for you here, Charlie."

"What d'you mean, you'll wait? I want you to

meet Léli. You two will like each other. Come along, Cat.''

The house was narrow, perhaps eighteen feet across, with a small leaded-glass window to the left of the turquoise door, a bay window to the right. Beyond the bay window, set at right angles to the house, was a high brick wall abloom with purple clematis.

''Notice something, Cat?'' Charlie lifted the brass owl that was the doorknocker and let it drop. ''No dogs. No cats. No kids. Not a living soul since we passed through those gates. Who the hell lives in these places?''

''Yuppies?''

''Even yuppies have kids. Besides, yuppies are passé. Get with it, Cat. Nobody says yuppie anymore.''

''I do. It's a good, descriptive word. Everybody knows exactly what you mean. And it's legitimate. It's in Webster's dictionary.''

''It is?''

''Yup.''

Charlie shot me a withering glance as the door opened barely wide enough for a woman in a white pantsuit to sidle through. She closed the door firmly behind her.

She was a chunky, solid young woman, with thickset shoulders, heavy breasts, and wide hips. Her black hair was skinned back from a broad face and hung in a long ponytail down her back. A pair of

gold crosses dangled from her fleshy, pierced earlobes. Her eyes, set deep above high cheekbones
flicked across my face and fastened on Charlie's.

"I'm Mr. Harwood," Charlie smiled at her. "I
believe Dr. Steinhauer is expecting me."

She didn't return the smile.

"Dr. Steinhauer can't see you." Her face was im-
passive, the ebony eyes unreadable. "She tried to
get out of bed and she hurt herself. I had to give her
a needle for the pain. She is asleep. She told me to
tell you she would call."

Charlie frowned, then tried the smile again. "And
you are...?"

For a moment I thought she wouldn't answer.
When she did, there was a hint of defiance in her
voice.

"I am Juanita Santos. Her nurse."

"Well, Miss Santos." Charlie's smile vanished
and he was suddenly Charles, intimidating and mas-
sively large. "I would like to see Dr. Steinhauer,
asleep or not."

Apprehension flickered briefly in her dark eyes.
She raised her hand and grasped the door handle.
Somehow, with that movement, her stolid body be-
came a barricade to the house.

Seconds ticked by, Charlie looming over her, she
staring stonily into his face.

Charlie capitulated.

"Well, then," he bit the words out. "*Por favor,*
would you see that Dr. Steinhauer gets these roses."

She snatched the florist box from him, opened the door no wider than she had the first time, and scuttled backward into the house. The turquoise door slammed in our faces. We heard a lock click into place, then another.

"Sonovabitch," Charlie said. "Let's go, Cat." He turned abruptly and walked down the path.

In the car, he snapped on his seat belt, waited until I had started the engine, then turned to me and asked, "Are you doing Beacon Mall tomorrow?"

"Yes."

"The vendor who sold you the Majorelle. You think he'll be there?"

"He was last week."

Charlie nodded. "I think we'll come and take a look at this guy," he said.

"Why?"

"Because something here is not kosher. If Léli was selling out, we'd be the first she'd call."

"Did she ever call you? After Aaron's funeral, I mean."

"Not right away. We tried getting her a couple of times, but there was never an answer. And then—you know the way time flits by, Cat—it was a couple of years later the phone rang on a Saturday afternoon. We were getting ready to close.

"It was Léli. She said, 'Charlie? I need your help.'"

Charlie was silent as we passed through the Court

gates. I glanced at him as I made the turn onto the main road. He was miles away, lost in thought.

"So then?" I prompted.

He shook his head.

"Sorry, Cat," he said. "So then we went to see her. The next morning. Sunday."

# SEVENTEEN

LÉLI'S HOUSE was one of those old stone places with three or four chimneys sticking up out of the roof and a wraparound veranda. Circular driveway, lots of tall trees and flowering shrubs. Well maintained. It was that kind of neighborhood.

The door to the house was the original. Thick beveled glass etched with floral baskets and framed in oak. The brass doorbell was a classic, the old type that clatters when the handle is twisted. Lovely.

A woman with short gray hair and granny glasses opened the door. A couple of seconds must have clicked by before we recognized her.

"That bad, huh?" Léli said.

She was dressed in a green sleeveless T-shirt and denim cutoffs. She was barefoot and she was thin. Not slim. Scrawny, the way old women get? Her hair looked as if it had been chopped off with garden shears. Her face had that powdery sort of paleness you see on old people. Fine wrinkles around the eyes, deeper wrinkles around the mouth. No makeup, not even lipstick. I looked at Rafe. This was *Léli?*

"Come in," she said. "I'm making apple pancakes."

We followed her into one of those huge, high-ceilinged old kitchens. It smelled of cinnamon and coffee. The kitchen table was set for three.

"Sit. Eat your grapefruit while I finish the pancakes."

She went to the stove, flipped the pancakes, and told us why she'd called for help.

"I've sold this place"—she waved the spatula at the walls—"and bought myself a town house you could probably squeeze into this kitchen. I've got a houseful of junk to get rid of, and I need your advice."

She looked at us, first at Rafe, then at me.

Neither of us said boo. I imagine Rafe was having the same problem I was having, trying to adjust Léli's husky, familiar voice with this...what the hell, it's what she was—this old woman. This stranger.

Rafe recovered first.

"When do you have to be out of here?"

"The end of the month."

"Two weeks? Not much time."

"I know." Léli turned back to the stove and scooped hot pancakes from the pan to a platter.

She brought the platter to the table, whisked away the grapefruit dishes and set them on the counter, and sat down at the table, pushing her glasses up from her nose to the top of her head and rubbing her eyes with the heels of her hands.

"Are you all right?" Rafe asked. He sounded more polite than concerned.

She dropped her hands. "I'm fine. Now."

Unexpectedly, she laughed, a genuine Léli giggle from the old days.

"You two," she said. "Nobody's ever going to accuse you of being inscrutable. If you think I look like hell now, you should have seen me a year ago."

She gestured at the pancakes. "Serve yourselves," she said, and told us what the past two years had been.

When Aaron came home to die, Léli took leave of absence from the hospital. A respectable time after the funeral, the hospital director phoned to ask when she planned to return. She postponed making a decision. A month later he called, and a month after that, politely insistent on an answer. They wanted her back.

"They may have called again, I don't know. By then I'd stopped answering the phone."

Léli made a wry face. "By then I'd stopped doing a lot of things. The only mail I opened was bills—usually not until they were at the final-notice stage. I stopped dyeing my hair. Who for? I didn't cook. Food didn't interest me. I drank a lot of wine. A *lot* of wine."

Léli pushed her plate away. She'd barely touched her pancake. She picked up her coffee mug and held it with both hands. Her nails were trimmed to the quick.

"One night I woke up," she continued. "It was four in the morning. I woke up wired and craving tomato juice. Ice cold. The more I tried not to think about it, the more I had to have it. Finally I threw on some clothes, drove to an all-night convenience store, and grabbed three large cans off the shelf. The man behind the counter had put down the morning paper he'd been reading, and I read the date while he rang up the sale. *May twenty-seventh*. I didn't even wait for my change. I raced home, with every nerve and muscle in my body jerking and twitching."

Léli looked at us, her dark eyes mocking, and for the first time I saw the old Léli.

"Here's where you get to think I'm a nut case," she said. "Or heading into senility."

"Why?" Rafe leaned forward, his voice soft, and I knew he'd seen her too. The real Léli.

She laughed. "Because I loathe tomato juice."

"Oh...?" Rafe prompted.

"May twenty-seventh was my sixty-fifth birthday. I think my body knew. Me, I didn't know one day from the next. If I hadn't wakened obsessed with the damn tomato juice, it would have been just another fuzzy day. What I think happened is my body said enough. Time to get on with it."

Rafe nodded. "It's possible."

"I think so. But I still think it was a peculiar way to go about telling me. Tomato juice?"

"Got your attention," Rafe said.

"Oh, yes. That it did." Léli set her coffee mug aside, put her elbows on the table, and rested her chin in palms of her hands, her face pensive.

"*That's* when you should have seen me," she said. "That morning. Dressed in clothing I'd dropped on the floor when I went to bed and put back on when I got out of bed. I couldn't have told you when I'd last bathed. My hair was a bird's nest. My teeth were gray, my toenails were yellow, and I was fifteen pounds skinnier than I am now. That's the revolting old bag I saw in the mirror on my sixty-fifth birthday."

She reached for her coffee mug, saw it was empty, and rose from the table. "Anybody want more coffee?" she asked.

Neither Rafe nor I wanted more.

Léli went to the stove and filled her cup, asking over her shoulder, "Do either of you know what the worst hours of the day are?"

Rafe shook his head, I said no.

"From four in the afternoon to midnight."

She returned to the table and sat down.

"I had no desire to go back to the hospital," she said. "I didn't need a job. What I needed was something to kill those hours. I volunteered at a storefront clinic. That was eight months ago. Now I put in six nights a week at three clinics, all of them in poor neighborhoods. My car has been broken into so often I stopped locking it. And I don't like driving at night. So I bought the town house. I can hop a bus to all three clinics."

"Makes sense," Rafe nodded. "Three clinics? You must like what you're doing."

Léli looked surprised. "Like? I'm useful. Maybe that was all I needed. To be of some use to somebody."

"Don't we all," Rafe said. "So. How can we be of some use to you?"

She smiled. "There's thirty years accumulation in this house. I can't take it with me. What do I do?"

"You sell it," Rafe said. "What else?"

"How? Who do I sell it to?"

"Have an estate sale."

"Uh," Léli grunted dubiously. "One, I don't know how. Two, I don't have the time. Three, I don't have the energy."

"Hire somebody."

"All right. Who?"

Rafe rose from the table. "Maybe we should take a look around, top to bottom. See what we're talking about here."

"Good idea." Léli pushed her chair back. "We can start in the attic."

It was a large house. Four levels. Attic, upstairs, main floor, basement. Léli and I dropped onto the living room sofa, three hours later, pooped. Rafe prowled around the room.

"What's in the boxes?" He put his hand on a stack of sealed cartons, all red-tabbed.

"Small stuff I packed myself. I didn't want the packers handling it."

"What kind of small stuff?"

"Aaron's collection. Mine. Things."

"What kind of things?" Rafe persisted.

"Does it matter?"

"Yes."

"If you say so." Léli frowned, concentrating. "Chelsea figurines we picked up in England. Belleek we bought in Ireland. The Meissen dinner set we bought from you. All the silver..."

"Sterling?"

"Yes."

"Go on."

"The crystal—"

"Good crystal or pinwheel crap?"

"Waterford."

Rafe nodded. "Go on."

"My jewelry," Léli said impatiently. "I don't wear it any longer but I don't think I'm ready to sell it. Does it really matter?"

"Yes. Anything else?"

Léli threw up her hands. "Lots more. I packed the things I want to keep. I don't remember all of it."

"You didn't keep a list?"

"No."

"Or photograph any of it?"

"No. Why would I?"

Rafe eyed the cartons. My stomach growled loudly.

Léli grinned at me. "Was that you? Are you hungry?"

"I'm always hungry at noon."

"Noon? Is it that late?" She stood up. "Let's go back to the kitchen. I made a big pot of bean soup yesterday."

We trotted back to the kitchen. Rafe and I sat down at the table. Léli bustled about. She set a large cast-iron pot on the stove, sliced a baguette, brought bowls to the table and sat down.

"Soup will be ready in a minute," she said to me, then to Rafe, "All right. You've seen it. What do I do?"

Rafe held up his right index finger.

"First," he said, "you do not, *do not* let the movers touch the cartons in the living room."

Léli's eyes widened. "Why not?"

"Because when the packers come tomorrow and see what you have in the rest of the house, some of those cartons are going to disappear in transit. Maybe all."

"But…" Léli shook her head, "they're insured. Aren't they?" she added uncertainly.

"Yes. They are. And when you put in a claim for a set of dishes, you're not going to get Meissen. Not even close."

"That's not nice." Léli frowned.

Rafe smiled. "No. But you'd be surprised how

often it happens. So you're going to leave those cartons right where they are, and when you're ready, Charlie and I will drive you and them down to the new place."

"You will?" Léli brightened. "Thank you. That would be wonderful. What about the rest of the stuff?"

Rafe leaned back in his chair and crossed his arms over his chest. "There we have a problem," he said.

"We do?"

"We do. Charlie and I came here as friends. Not dealers. There are a lot of things we'd like to buy."

Léli tilted her head. "Give me a for instance."

"Well...the two Royal Dux figurines."

"How much are they worth?"

"Between two and three thousand dollars. That's what we might get for them. It isn't what we could pay for them."

"What else?"

Rafe dropped his arms. "I lost track, Léli. A tapestry. A folio stand. The Windsor chair you're sitting on."

Léli rose from the Windsor chair. She went to the stove and stirred the soup thoughtfully.

"Why don't we do it this way," she said. "You come and cart off whatever you want. Does that solve the problem?"

"Not entirely," Rafe said.

"Why not?"

"Because we can't pay you what the things are worth, and we won't lie to you."

"You don't have to lie to me. You take what you want, sell it, and give me a third of whatever you sell it for."

Rafe shook his head. "We'll give you half."

"Sorry, Rafe. It's my way or no way."


"THAT WAS seven years ago." Charlie unbuckled his seat belt. We were parked in front of Canterbury House. "We've kept in touch, mostly by phone."

"You don't see her?"

"She's too busy. The last time we saw her was when she bought the Majorelle." Charlie frowned. "Christ Almighty, Cat, that was over a year ago! Where the hell does time go?"

I glanced at my watch.

"Speaking of time. If I want to beat the traffic…"

"Oh. Sure. Sorry."

Charlie opened the door and got out, leaning down to look in through the car window.

"Thanks, Cat. We'll see you Sunday at Beacon Mall."

# EIGHTEEN

"IT'S GOING TO BE a stinker."

Helen, one of the vendors from my old flea market days, leaned against her van, parked next to mine in the Beacon Mall lot. She swiped at her damp forehead with the back of her wrist.

"I'm getting too old for this," she groaned. "It's gotta be ninety degrees and it isn't even seven o'clock yet."

"Well, maybe the air-conditioning will bring out a good crowd," I offered small comfort. "Nobody will want to work in the garden in this heat."

"We hope." Helen sighed. "But let me tell you, the first customer who says I must love doing this is going to get slapped upside the head with my Spode coffeepot."

"Or the one who thinks we meet such interesting people?"

"Sure we do." Helen laughed. "Or the one who says it's something to do on a Sunday?"

"Ah, well. As long as they buy."

"I guess." Helen reached into the van and slid a carton toward the door. "One more year, Catherine. Ben'll be sixty-five. With his pension coming in I'll be able to cut back. Maybe do only Finney's in the summer. If I live that long.''

"How is he? Ben?"

"How can he be?" Helen's shrug was one of resignation. "He's had two minor strokes since the big one. His left side's useless, and he has trouble talking. He tries so damn hard. Then he gets frustrated and cries like a kid.''

"That's rough, Helen. He was such a strong, sweet man.''

"Yeah. Well. Them's the breaks.'' Helen lifted the heavy carton from the van. "Back to the salt mines, kiddo.''

I grabbed the last box from Rena's van and followed her into the air-conditioned mall, perspiration trickling down my nose and from my armpits to my waist.

Old Sam hadn't arrived yet, which was unusual. Normally he was first man in. A couple of dealers and Shifty George dawdled idly across from me, waiting for him.

I busied myself with setting up and selling, and it wasn't until almost nine o'clock, when other vendors began placing odds and ends in the empty space across from mine, where Old Sam should have been, that I was aware he was still missing.

The morning rush ended, the dealers departed. I was settling into my chair with coffee, a muffin, and a paperback when Mike appeared. He sidled around the tables.

"Where's Old Sam?" he demanded.

"How would I know?" I said defensively, taken aback by his peremptory tone. "Why?"

"Because I know who he is."

"Great. Who is he?"

"Got any more of that coffee?"

I filled the thermos top and handed it to him. He sipped and made a face.

"There's no sugar in it," he complained.

"I don't take sugar. If I'd known you were coming I'd have brought some. Want a muffin?"

"Is it one of those bran things you make?"

"Yes."

"You know I hate bran muffins."

"Too bad. Who is he? Old Sam."

Mike dragged a plastic milk crate from beneath the table and sat down on it.

"It was driving me crazy," he said. "I never forget a face. Names sometimes. Not faces. And I was positive I knew that face."

"Excuse me a second, Mike."

A customer handed me two paperbacks, and two dollars. I bagged the books, thanked the man, and sat down again.

"You knew the face," I prompted Mike.

"I was lying in bed, wondering where the hell I knew the guy from. I was picturing him in my mind, the way he was at the flea market, talking to his daughter. *Daughter* led to *son*. Then it hit me—Sam.

Son. *Samson.* Phil Samson, for Christ's sake. Old Sam used to be Philip K. Samson.''

"Who was Philip K. Samson?"

"It was the lisp that threw me off." Mike finished his coffee and handed me the thermos top. "I figured I'd remember anybody who sounded like Bogart. But he didn't have the lisp when I interviewed him."

"You interviewed him? Old Sam?"

"Twenty-five years ago. At least that. Phil was a hotshot back then."

"What sort of hotshot?"

"I was doing a column on charity. Where-the-money-goes crap? I interviewed two or three fund-raisers. Philip K. Samson was one of them. I remember him as a pretty smooth talker, but what the hell, they all were."

Mike's gaze shifted. He gestured past me with a tilt of his head. "You've got a customer," he said.

After assuring a young woman that the bracelet she liked was sterling, the number 925 indicates sterling, and having her decide she'd think about it, I was back in my chair.

"Go on," I said. "What happened to Philip K. Samson? How did he get to be Old Sam?"

"He made a mistake. He was caught skimming."

"Skimming? You mean stealing?"

Mike shrugged. "I doubt he thought of it as stealing. They all did it. Phil's mistake was who he did it to. He was raising money for an Irish Catholic athletic association, a bunch of cops and soccer players and wrestlers and boxers, and every one of them as Irish as Mother Machree. When they found out he was diddling them, they took him to court. When they lost they took him into a dark alley.''

''They beat him up?''

''Up, down, and sideways.'' Mike nodded. ''And I bet that's when he acquired the lisp.''

''That's awful.'' I looked at the space opposite mine, where Old Sam should have been. Philip K. Samson. *Old Phil?*

''He gave up fund-raising?'' I asked.

''It gave him up. Too many people knew.''

''That he was skimming?''

''He was acquitted. Whether he was skimming, nobody cared. It was his lack of judgment that finished him. Boondoggling the Irish brotherhood? He was the local joke for a few weeks, and that you don't survive.''

''Did you think he was guilty?''

''Probably. It was a long time ago. I don't remember thinking about it one way or another.'' Mike gestured with his head. ''She's back.''

''I really do want the bracelet,'' the young woman said, ''It's marked twenty dollars, but all I have with me is eighteen dollars.'' She hesitated, her smile bashful. ''Would you...I mean, I don't suppose you'd let it go for eighteen dollars, would you?''

I would. She thanked me, several times, paid me

in small bills and a handful of change, fastened the bracelet around her wrist, and walked away, delighted with me, her purchase, and herself.

Suddenly, there was a surge of humanity, a flea market phenomenon for which there is no logical explanation. One minute a bowling ball can be hurled down the aisle without striking a living soul, the next the place is as teeming as an island port of call when a cruise ship docks.

Charlie and Rafe arrived as I was refolding a beautiful lace tablecloth, underpriced at thirty dollars.

An overbearing matron and her mother had measured and dickered over it for ten minutes. They had offered fifteen, raised it to eighteen and thrown it in a heap when I wouldn't accept less than twenty-five.

Charlie shouldered his way between two customers, a man and woman dressed in identical pink tank tops.

"Cat? Which vendor?" he asked.

"The man with the beard. Right across from the deli."

Charlie nodded. "See you later."

He and Rafe edged away from the table.

"Excuse me." The woman in the pink top waved to get my attention. "The tablecloth. Did I hear you say you'd let it go for twenty-five?"

"Yes. Would you like to see it?"

"Oh, we've seen it," she smiled. "We were just waiting for that woman to make up her mind. We'll take it. There are no rips or stains we didn't notice are there?''

I assured her the cloth was in perfect condition, folded it into a bag, thanked her, and went on to the next customer, a man waiting patiently to pay four dollars for an old wooden spirit level. I was making change when Mike nudged me.

''Look who's back,'' he muttered.

It was *that* woman and her mother. She eyed me through the lower half of her bifocals.

''I've decided to take the tablecloth at twenty-five dollars,'' she announced. ''Where is it?''

''I'm sorry, it's sold.''

Her thin brows rose indignantly. ''It can't be sold,'' she snapped. ''I was here just a minute ago.''

''I'm sorry,'' I repeated, ''I sold it just a minute ago.''

Mike chuckled as the irate pair stalked away. I laughed with him.

''There you go,'' I said. ''That's every vendor's favorite comeback for a chintzy customer. *Sorry, it's sold.*''

With lunch hour approaching, the after-church crowd had thinned to a few locals drifting aimlessly, taking shelter from the oppressive heat outdoors. Two or three turned to stare, idly rude, at Rafe's face as he and Charlie came striding back to my table.

''Do you know him?'' I asked.

''We've seen him at auctions,'' Rafe said.

"He has some nice pieces."

Rafe nodded. "Yes. He does. But I don't think he's very knowledgeable. His pricing doesn't make sense. He's put a Royal Crown Derby price on a trashy new Capo di Monte piece and he's practically giving away a Waterford decanter. I'm surprised nobody picked up on it."

"You didn't buy it?"

"It's only about fifteen years old. Too new for us."

"Did you mention the Majorelle?"

"We'll talk to Léli first. He has a sterling kiddush cup on his table. It looks very much like one we sold to Aaron a few years ago."

"You think it might be the same one?"

Rafe shrugged. "I couldn't say for sure. We'll have to check out Aaron's collection. How are you doing with the sewing table?"

"I haven't found the right silk yet. I'll keep looking, but if I don't find a good piece I might have to use a linen damask. Are you in a rush?"

"Not really. We picked up a very nice demilune dwarf commode that needs work. Do you want to take it on now or would you rather wait until you finish the sewing table?"

"Now, I think. I haven't stripped the sewing table yet. I could do both at once. Okay if I pick it up this week?"

"Fine." Rafe scanned Rena's table. "Is there anything for us here?"

Charlie grasped Rafe's arm. "No, I've already looked. Come on, Rafe. Let's go. I'm hungry."

"You're always hungry."

"I'm a growing boy." Charlie released Rafe's arm and turned to Mike. "We're going to the Pancake House," he said. "Why don't you come along?"

"Maybe I will." Mike pushed himself to his feet. "Do you think Sam will be in today, Cat?"

"I doubt it. He wouldn't come this late in the day. We'll be packing in a couple of hours."

"I wonder if he showed up for dinner with his daughter on Saturday night. What was her name again?"

"Sandy. I'm sure he did. She was pretty sore at him."

"If he didn't, he's dead meat today."

IT WASN'T UNTIL next morning we learned Philip K. Samson had been dead meat for three days.

# NINETEEN

### ROADSIDE BODY IDENTIFIED

The body of a man found dead on a road near Lake Echo on Friday has been identified as that of Philip K. Samson. Police believe Samson may have picked up a hitchhiker who killed him before fleeing with Samson's van. The van was found abandoned in the east end of the city late Saturday.

ONE PARAGRAPH on page six of the second section of the Monday morning *Gazette*. I read it twice, trying to put Old Sam's face on it, unsuccessfully. Philip K. Samson was a stranger. I picked up the phone and called Rena.

"I know," she said. "Sam's daughter is here."

"Sandy? She's there?"

"You know Sandy?"

"Not really. I met her, that's all. If she's there…" I hesitated. "I was planning to pass by with your money. I sold your Doulton jug at Finney's and I had a good day at Beacon. Would you rather I came tomorrow?"

"No. It's all right. Come today."

SANDY MET ME at the door.

She was dressed in the same yellow sundress she had worn to Finney's on Friday. Without the straw hat and the sunglasses she was somehow less sophisticated, plainer. Her light brown hair, cut very short, had been given no more than a hasty finger-combing. She wore no makeup. Her eyes were puffy and red-rimmed.

"Come in," she said. The ghost of a smile flickered, disappeared. "We're in the kitchen."

I followed her down the hall.

Rena sat at the kitchen table, looking better than I expected, her hands circling a coffee mug. Her eyes had lost their dullness, and there was color in her cheeks.

"Hello, Catherine," she said. "Coffee?"

"Please." I drew back the chair opposite her and sat down.

Sandy took a mug from the cupboard. Pouring coffee for me, she resumed the subject that had obviously been under discussion before I arrived.

"Rena," she said, "I'm telling you, Daddy would never have picked up a hitchhiker."

"The police say he must have," Rena said, a hint of mulishness in her tone. "How else would..."

"No." Sandy shook her head vehemently. "Not in a million years. Half his stock was in that van. And he always carried a lot of cash." She turned to me. "You heard him, Catherine. He was going to

Lake Echo to buy out an estate. Isn't that what he said?''

I nodded. "That's what he said."

Sandy brought my coffee to the table and sat down beside Rena. She frowned at me, her mouth tight. "Do you think he'd have picked up a hitch-hiker?" she asked.

"I don't know. I don't think so. Maybe he stopped to help a car in trouble on the road?"

"Daddy wouldn't do that. He doesn't know anything about cars. And he's always been scared stiff of being robbed. He'd drive around any trouble."

"Did you tell that to the police?"

"Of course I told them. At least ten times. I told them Daddy would *never* pick somebody up off the road."

"What did they say?"

"I don't think they listened." Sandy blinked rapidly. "All they seemed to care about was getting me to look at...to see if..."

"How did they find you? I mean, how did they know who to contact? The newspaper said it was an 'unidentified body.'''

"They didn't find me," Sandy said. "I called them. I went to Daddy's apartment on Saturday morning. When I got there, the morning paper was still on the doormat. The van wasn't in his parking space, so I figured he'd gone out early. I prepared supper and waited, and when he hadn't come home by midnight I phoned all the hospitals and then the police.''

She drew a ragged breath.

''After I had identified…afterward…they told me the hitchhiker had Daddy's keys and I should have the locks changed. And that was it. Thank you. Good-bye. We'll let you know when we have something.''

''Did you have the locks changed?''

''Right away. Sunday morning.'' Sandy frowned. ''Was that only yesterday? It feels like ages ago.''

''According to the newspapers, he was killed on Friday.''

Sandy nodded. ''But they're wrong about the hitchhiker.'' Her jaw set stubbornly. ''So are the police. I know Daddy. He wouldn't…'' Her voice trailed away.

''Maybe he had car trouble himself,'' I suggested.

''He couldn't have. The van was driven back to town.''

''Sandy, something—or somebody—got him out of his van. And if you're right about him, it had to be somebody he knew. Either at Lake Echo or on the road. Have you any idea who he was going to see at Lake Echo?''

Sandy shook her head.

''There was nothing in his pockets. His wallet was gone. And there was nothing in the van. No notes, nothing.''

''Maybe the police are checking Lake Echo.''

"I don't think they're checking anything," Sandy said bitterly. "Hitchhiker. Case closed."

"Sandy." Rena had been listening silently, sipping her coffee. She set her mug down firmly. "It happens all the time. People pick up hitchhikers who rob them. Even kill them. You must accept that the police may be right."

"No."

Sandy's hands curled into fists. She glared at Rena, more in childish defiance than in anger. Rena's shoulders lifted in a shrug of resignation. They appeared to have come full circle.

I reached into my bag for Rena's envelope.

"Your money." I handed the envelope to her. "And a list of what was sold. I'm going to need new stock, Rena."

She took the envelope, grimacing.

"I haven't had the energy to look into the boxes in the basement," she said. "Go with what we have this week. I plan to do garage sales this weekend. You'll have something new for next week."

"Garage sales? Are you sure you're well enough?"

"Well enough to go around to some garage sales for a few hours. If I don't buy now I'll have nothing this winter."

"Then you'll need your van."

"No. Frank will drive me in his car."

Rena glanced at Sandy. "There is something you could do, Catherine, if you will," she said. "Sandy needs money. Would you consider taking a couple of Sam's boxes to Finney's and to Beacon this week?''

"Of course. If it's all right with you, it makes no difference to me what I sell. Where do I get the boxes?''

"You can pick them up at Sam's apartment. Sandy says all the stock he had in the van was smashed to pieces.''

"All of it?''

"Everything,'' Sandy put in angrily. "Every single box was opened, and everything in every box was smashed to bits. Deliberately. Does that make sense to you, Catherine? Does it make sense for some passing hitchhiker to—''

"Sandy, please,'' Rena said wearily. "Nothing we say or do will bring Sam back. Enough for today. Please.''

Sandy grimaced but she let it go. She scribbled Old Sam's address and phone number on a scrap of paper and handed it to me.

"I've taken the week off,'' she said. "I'll be there for the next few days. When can you come?''

"Let's make it tomorrow morning. At ten?''

Sandy agreed, and I asked Rena for the use of her phone. I called Canterbury House. Charlie answered.

"I'm halfway into town,'' I said. "Can I pick up the commode if I come the rest of the way?''

"Whenever. Cat? Did you hear about Sam?''

"Yes. See you in about twenty minutes, Charlie.''

# TWENTY

IF, GOD FORBID, I ever succumb to the urge to have an antique shop of my own, it will have to be a carbon copy of Canterbury House or forget it.

Rafe—Charlie credits him entirely—has managed to avoid the cluttered effect of hundreds of objects overwhelming a confined space and has created instead an atmosphere of serenity and elegance.

Lighting is soft and indirect, provided by tinted bulbs in the mirror-backed glass shelving lining the walls, and by antique lamps among artful arrangements of furniture. The air is cool and faintly lemon-scented. The background music, Segovia today, is muted.

Charlie and Rafe were at the rear, rearranging a display of Hummel figurines. Both agreed Old Sam would never have picked up a hitchhiker.

"Never," Rafe said. "Sam carried too much cash and too much valuable merchandise."

"He did?" I said, surprised. "I've never seen anything so great on his tables."

"You wouldn't," Rafe said. "He never put his good stuff out at flea markets. Sam's flea market booths were his—I guess you could call them his headquarters."

Headquarters. I told Charlie and Rafe of my suspicions about Old Sam.

Rafe shook his head. "He wasn't selling drugs."

"You sound very sure."

"I am sure. Sam never sold drugs."

"So what was he selling? How could he get folding money for dog-eared Harlequin paperbacks that were overpriced at thirty-five cents?"

"He sold baby laxative."

"He sold *what?*"

"Powdered baby laxative. It's used for cutting cocaine."

I stared at them speechlessly, first at Charlie, then at Rafe. Both looked mildly amused.

Rafe placed the last Hummel on the shelf and slid the glass door closed.

"Let's take a break," he said.

He seated himself at the partners desk and gestured me to the chair opposite. Charlie dropped onto an Empire rose-tapestried chaise. He hooked a petit-point footstool with his booted toe, dragged it closer, and put his feet up on it.

"You know Sebastian Resende, don't you, Cat?" Rafe asked.

"I know who he is. The hole-in-the-wall shop on Park?"

Rafe nodded. "Antero Antiques."

"Ninety percent junk. Does he ever sell anything?"

"Only about a thousand bucks a day," Charlie said.

"Are you kidding?" I looked at Rafe. "He is kidding, isn't he?"

"No. He's not," Rafe said. "Sebastian imports powdered baby laxative by the barrel from Italy, bags it, and sells it for thirty-five dollars a bag."

"Is it legal?"

"There's no law against selling baby laxative. What happens after it leaves the shop is illegal, but that isn't Sebastian's problem."

"Do the police know what he's doing?"

"Sure they know," Charlie said. "They've asked him to cease and desist, which is about all they can do."

Rafe smiled. "Every once in a while, when they have nothing better to do, they set up surveillance on the shop to identify the buyers. It's never worked. Sebastian can smell them. He warns his customers off until it's over."

"He came in here one day," Charlie said, "all righteous indignation. The fuckin' fuzz were cutting into his profits. He wanted an alternative outlet, a clean one. Namely us."

"You? Here?"

"Hey," Charlie's brows arched. "We were tempted."

"Ignore him, Cat," Rafe said. "We never considered it. Sebastian is robbed at least once a month, the last time with a knife at his throat. He writes it off as a business expense. Next thing we heard he had a vendor in every flea market. He outbids for space number thirty-five and sets his sales reps up with thirty-five-dollar bags and a box of thirty-five-cent paperbacks." Rafe shrugged. "Sebastian has a flair for the dramatic."

"So Old Sam isn't the only one?"

"Hell, no," Charlie said. "Sam only got into the act a couple of months ago. He jumped the waiting list."

Rafe laughed. "Tell Cat how he did it," he said.

"He jumped Sebastian's sister." Charlie chortled.

"Sebastian brought his sister over from Portugal this spring," Rafe explained. "You've seen Sebastian, haven't you, Cat?"

"Not that I remember."

"He's a bandy-legged little guy with oily black hair and a scraggly mustache, who always smells of garlic. And Sofia is enough like him to be his twin. Including the mustache. Sam probably had to close his eyes and hold his nose, but I bet it was the best-paid servicing he'd ever done."

My nose wrinkled with distaste. "That's sick," I said.

"Come on, Cat," Charlie snorted. "Sam was a hustler. He wheeled and dealed all over town. Last time he was in here he had a hundred thousand dollars' worth of stuff in his pocket. A watch, alone, worth forty thousand bucks."

"What kind of watch is worth forty thousand dollars?" I asked.

"A 1939 gold moon-phase Patek Phillippe," Rafe said. "He had it on consignment. And maybe that's what got him killed. He had something valuable somebody wanted very badly."

"Badly enough to kill for?"

"I could probably think of at least four people who would do it," Rafe's said drily.

"You're not serious," I said.

"Half serious. Two people."

I had a sudden mental image of the fat man at Finney's.

"Do you know a big, sloppy man with a shaggy red beard? I think his name is Leo—"

"Tolstoy," Charlie and Rafe said together.

"Tolstoy?"

"Leo claims he's a direct descendent." Rafe shrugged. "He could be. Who knows? Or cares. Leo's a slob with a very short fuse, but he knows his stuff. Why do you ask?"

"I saw him yelling at Old Sam out at Finney's."

Charlie laughed. "Yelling? That's all? For Leo, that's being friendly."

"It didn't look very friendly to me."

"You've never heard the Leo-Phoebe story?"

"No."

"You must know her, Cat. Phoebe Pennington."

"Is she the one with the shop in Kirkland? Penny's Attic? Black hair, tall and thin? Fortyish?"

"That's Pheeb," Charlie nodded. "Her shop flopped about a year ago, but she still does the shows. Her booth was across from ours at the Kingston show last fall."

"I remember. She had a nice needlepoint pole screen."

"It was probably Leo's. Apparently Phoebe had somewhere between four and five thousand worth of his merchandise on consignment in her shop when she went belly-up. She stalled him for months, Leo trying to collect money or merchandise, whichever, yelling and screaming, but not getting nasty about it. He knew things were rough."

"Yelling and screaming don't count as nasty?"

Charlie laughed. "Hey," he said. "That's Leo's shtick. Leo's the Mad Russian. And Phoebe's no thin-skinned little chickadee, you know. They got along."

"So what happened?"

"What happened is, Phoebe sold a Chiparus figure for thirteen grand to an out-of-town dealer on Friday night, while she was setting up for the Westmount show. You know what shows are like, Cat. Anything over two thousand goes out the door, everybody knows about it. Nobody begrudged her. But she made two mistakes. She was so damn pleased with herself she told one of the dealers she'd bought it for eighty-five bucks from a little old lady going into a nursing home. That was mistake numero uno, and Phoebe is old enough to have known better. If one dealer knows about the sale, everybody knows.''

I nodded. ''And mistake number two?''

''That was the biggy. Leo heard about the Chiparus, of course. You know the circuit, Cat. It's the same as the flea markets. Somebody farts at Finney's on Friday, it's an old stink at Beacon by Sunday. Leo probably knew ten minutes after the sale was a done deal. He came in next morning, Saturday, the first day of the show, presented himself at Pheeb's table, and asked for his money. Asked nicely, too. I don't think he expected any argument.''

Charlie paused for dramatic effect.

''Phoebe stood there with her bare face hanging out,'' he continued, ''and told him she didn't have the money. She told him she hadn't made a sale yet.''

Rafe chimed in.

''You have to get the picture, Cat,'' he said. ''It's early. The customers haven't started coming in. The dealers are hanging around with nothing better to do, and they hear Phoebe. Don't forget, everybody knows the whole story. They know she's lying. Most of them know Leo. Everybody freezes.''

''Including us,'' Charlie grinned. ''It was like the air was sucked out of the place for a couple of seconds there. Then old Leo bellowed. No yelling, no screaming. He bellowed like a goddam bull. I swear, we actually heard the crystal goblets on our table ringing. He grabbed the edge of Phoebe's table and raised it to shoulder level and every damn thing on that table slid down and hit the marble floor. You've never seen anything like it. All the dealers were standing like cigar-store Indians, wincing at the crashing and smashing, but grinning too, because there was something so goddamn awesome about it, and the stuff wasn't theirs anyway. Then Leo let the table drop and walked out without saying a word.''

"Phoebe tried to sue," Rafe added. "But she couldn't find a single witness to back her up. Nobody saw nuttin'. She had to eat the loss. So did Leo, of course. But it put her out of business. Him, it helped. Nobody messes with Leo.''

I looked from Rafe's one-sided smile to Charlie's single glinting golden eye.

"Old Sam's van," I said. "Everything in it was smashed. Every box was opened, and everything inside was systematically smashed. Would Leo be capable of doing something like that?''

Rafe and Charlie glanced at one another. Rafe nodded.

"Yes," Charlie agreed. "If he was pissed off enough.''

"Pissed off enough, do you think he would be capable of killing Old Sam?''

"No," Rafe said.

"Yes," said Charlie.

# TWENTY-ONE

OLD SAM'S PLACE was in a four-unit apartment building. Two up, two down, with P. SAMSON typed on a white card in the slot beside a pearl button with a 3 engraved on it.

I pressed the button and stood with my hand on the knob of the interior door, waiting for the lock to be released. As the buzzer sounded, the street door opened. A pretty young black woman, her hair in tight cornrows, her arms encircling a pair of brown paper grocery bags, stepped into the foyer.

"Hold it for me please?" she said cheerfully. "If I put these down I'll never be able to pick them up again."

I held the door for her. She passed through and waited for me to follow.

"Thanks." There was a sheen of perspiration on her upper lip and forehead. She repositioned the two bags to sit more comfortably on her hip bones.

"I should have asked for plastic bags with handles," she smiled. But I can't seem to decide which is worse. Killing trees for the paper or churning out plastic that doesn't biodegrade."

"I know. I haven't made up my mind either. Why

don't you give me one of those bags? I'm going upstairs too.''

"Are you sure?" She eyed me doubtfully. "They're pretty heavy."

"Don't worry. I'm stronger than I look."

She laughed, a lovely, husky sound, and released one bag with a sigh of relief. We mounted the stairs together.

"That's a terrible thing that happened to Mr. Samson," she said. "Poor Sandy."

"Yes." I had a fleeting second of difficulty connecting her "Mr. Samson" to Old Sam. "Did you know him well?"

"Not all that well." She glanced back at me. "My kids liked him. I work nights, and he was always sort of there if they needed him, you know? He was a good neighbor. A nice man."

We reached a small landing where two heavily varnished doors faced each other; on one was a brass numeral three, on the other a four. She set her bag down on the tiled floor, took the other from me, and withdrew a set of keys from the pocket of her jeans.

"Thank you. My aching back thanks you," she said.

I heard the door to number 3 open behind me and Sandy stepped out on to the landing.

"Hi, Sandy," the pretty young woman said. "I'm so sorry for your loss. Your father was a nice man."

"Thank you, Ann-Marie." Sandy glanced back

and forth between us, her expression mildly curious. "Hi, Catherine."

"We met downstairs," Ann-Marie explained. She fit her key into the lock. "By the way," she said. "Some man was trying to get into your father's apartment the other day."

Sandy looked at me with startled eyes.

"When was this?" I asked.

"Sunday. Sunday evening. Around seven o'clock."

"What did he look like?" I asked.

"I didn't see him. I'd already left for work. The kids told me they saw a man with a bunch of keys trying to get into the apartment."

"I had the locks changed," Sandy said.

Ann-Marie unlocked her apartment door, swung it wide, and set her bag of groceries down on the floor inside. She turned back for the second bag.

"That's what I figured," she said, nodding. "Look, Sandy. If there's anything you need, ask. Okay?"

"Thanks. I will."

"Take care, then." Ann-Marie flashed us a smile and disappeared into her apartment.

I followed Sandy into Old Sam's living room.

Most flea-marketers live with their stock. Everything they buy comes into the house. If they don't own vans in which they can leave some of their stock it all gets unloaded into their homes or apartments. Eventually every room is cluttered with stacked boxes, every closet crammed with cartons, every surface is piled with pieces waiting to be cleaned, repaired, priced, or packed.

I've known one or two dealers who have successfully confined their merchandise to a limited area of the house, but for most it's a losing battle. The stuff is like a creeping mudslide; it overflows, filling every drawer and shelf and nook and cranny.

Sam's place was no different.

We stepped into the living room, not large to begin with. It was made even smaller by a wall of stacked plastic milk cartons filled with newspaper-wrapped objects. There were cardboard cartons along the window wall. An old air conditioner droned and rattled in the window, dripping moisture, blowing cool air but failing to dissipate the apartment's stale smell.

Several small pieces of furniture—a smokestand, a tall *étagère,* a longcase clock—narrowed the hall leading to the rest of the apartment.

"I don't even know where to start," Sandy gestured helplessly. "I've packed all Dad's clothes to give to the Salvation Army. The kitchen's no problem. But all this, I don't know. And the bedroom's just as bad."

"Not to panic." I dropped my handbag onto a chair. "How much time do we have?"

"Time? You mean today?"

"Not today. How much time do you have to get everything out of here? Out of the apartment."

"Oh." Sandy's face cleared. "The landlord said the rent is paid until September."

"Good. We should be able to get rid of your father's stuff by then. What about the furniture? Are you going to keep any of it?"

Sandy shook her head. "I live in a two-bedroom apartment with three other girls, so you can imagine. There's nothing here I want anyway."

"Okay. We'll worry about the furniture later. Let's get three boxes together for this weekend."

Sandy pointed to two boxes on the couch. "Those were on the kitchen table. Maybe they were the ones Dad was planning to take to Beacon on Sunday. Do you think?"

"Could be. Let's have a look."

Sandy took one box, I took the other. I began unpacking the top layer, unwrapping a pair of gilded plaster busts, one a frowning Chopin, the other a sour-faced Haydn. A blue Delft windmill. Some pink Depression glass.

Typical flea market crap. I rewrapped everything, closed the box, and went to choose one of the cartons piled under the windows.

"There are no prices on these things," Sandy said. "He must have just bought them."

She had cleared the coffee table and unpacked her box onto its surface. I glanced. Then I took a closer look. I set the carton I was holding down on the floor and went to kneel beside the coffee table.

"Wow," I said softly. Rafe was right. Old Sam hadn't taken the good stuff to flea markets.

"What?" Sandy asked.

"I don't think your father meant to take these things to any flea market," I said. "I think these are pieces he sold out of his pocket."

"Out of his pocket?" Sandy looked at me blankly. "What does that mean?"

"It means your father probably had antique dealers lined up for these things." I picked up an ornate, gilt-framed, rose-painted porcelain box. "This is Wave Crest, Sandy. It's probably listed at around two hundred dollars. If not more."

I replaced the Wave Crest on the table and picked up an ivory box containing a half dozen small figures.

"These funny little things are netsukes," I continued. "One hundred dollars minimum. Each. If they're signed they can run into the thousands. The little Toby jugs? They're Royal Doulton Tiny's. At least a hundred each. The opera glasses, the patch box, the Victorian card case, some of the other things I'd have to do some research, but this isn't the usual run of flea market junk, Sandy. These are antique-shop pieces."

Sandy eyed the objects on the table, an expression of distress on her face. She looked close to tears.

"Does that mean you can't sell them at the flea market?"

"Of course we can," I assured her, startled by

her reaction. I had expected gleeful smiles. "The dealers will swarm like ants at a picnic. They won't buy if they can't make money, so you'll have to be prepared to give them a good discount. If you'd rather wait, we can price the pieces close to list and hold out for collectors."

"I can't wait," Sandy said, desperation in her voice. "I need money now. The police are releasing the—Daddy's body this week. I have to arrange...there has to be some kind of funeral. Until I can sell the van, I've got exactly forty-six dollars in the bank."

"What about Old...your father's...money?"

"The only bank statement I've found shows a balance of eighteen dollars."

"That doesn't mean anything, Sandy. He dealt in cash."

"There was no money in the van. His wallet was gone."

"Forget the van." I pushed myself to my feet, both knees cracking audibly. "Have you searched in here?"

"Here? Wouldn't he have taken his money with him? He was going to Lake Echo to buy."

"He'd have taken only buying money with him."

"Oh. Do you think there's more?"

"There has to be. He's been dealing in cash for years. He's certainly not going to carry all of it around with him. Somewhere in this place is his cash cache.'' I smiled at her, ''Sorry, Sandy, I couldn't resist.''

Sandy frowned uncertainly.

''He probably kept his cashbox hidden in here somewhere,'' I continued, faintly abashed, ''That's where the money is.''

''Where would I find it?'' Sandy said helplessly. She eyed the stacked boxes. ''I wouldn't even know where to begin.''

''Ignore this stuff.'' I waved away the cartons. ''This is stock. Have you looked in the freezer?''

''The freezer?''

''The freezer compartment of the fridge. That's where Rena keeps hers. Stashed in a hollowed-out loaf of pumpernickel.''

I resisted saying the dough was in the bread, and I made no reference to cold cash. Or to frozen assets. Wrong person. Wrong time. Wrong place.

Also, not funny.

''Be sure to check everything,'' I said. ''Don't pack or throw out anything without going over it thoroughly. The money could be anywhere, Sandy. One vendor I knew kept her cash in the hem of her living room drapes. Check carefully.''

''I will,'' Sandy said dubiously. ''But why wouldn't they keep it in the bank?''

''Taxes. Secretiveness. Whatever. Flea-marketers just aren't your average nine-to-fivers, Sandy. They don't like showing up in a computer somewhere.''

I was surprised at how little she knew about her father's activities. Feeling no overpowering compulsion to educate her, I pressed on.

"All right. Here's what I suggest we do. We'll cut prices to the bone on the junk and take it all to Finney's. It should go quickly; there's some halfway decent stuff here. The good pieces we'll take to Beacon on Sunday. We'll aim for the dealers there and give them a discount they can live with. How does that sound to you?"

"Whatever you think." Sandy reached into the carton beside her. "There are some boxes of jewelry in here. Do you want them too?"

I shook my head. "I'm not good on jewelry. Rena knows a lot more than I do. She'll know how to price it. Pack them separately, and I'll drop them off on my way home."

"I'll take them with me," Sandy said. "Rena asked me to stay with her for a couple of days."

"Fine. Then let's get busy."

We packed three cartons, two for Finney's, one for Beacon, and carried them down to my car.

The noon sun had turned the street into a brick oven. I opened all four car doors and the back gate to release the suffocating heat from the interior. Waiting for the breeze, sultry as it was, to move through the car, I asked Sandy how many people had keys to Old Sam's apartment.

"Me. Daddy, of course. And Rena." She brushed sweat-dampened hair from her forehead. "Catherine? Did Rena ever tell you why they split up?''

"Why who split up?"

"Daddy and Rena."

"Your father? Rena?" I gaped at her, truly dumb-founded. "I didn't know they were ever together."

"They were together almost two years. I even thought they might get married or something." Sandy frowned, looking like a perplexed child.

"When did they split up?"

"This spring. Boom, suddenly they're barely speaking. When Daddy took the space next to Rena at Finney's, I thought maybe they'd get back to-gether, but it didn't happen. Daddy wouldn't talk about it. And I didn't have the nerve to ask Rena. I thought you might know."

"I'm sorry, Sandy. I really don't."

I walked around the car, closing the far doors, and then got in. Looking up at Sandy through the open window, I told her to keep Old Sam's apartment locked when she was inside.

"Why?"

I started the car. "Somebody has already tried to get in. Better safe than sorry. Keep the door locked. And keep the chain on. Okay?"

Sandy nodded, I raised my hand to wave then drove away.

Rena and Old Sam?

Sonovagun.

# TWENTY-TWO

I SPENT MOST OF Wednesday slashing prices on the mediocre flea market items in the two cartons I had brought back from Old Sam's. Which probably brought them down to what he had initially paid for them. Or less. I could almost hear Old Sam's howls of anguish.

Too bad.

I repacked the cartons and carried them out to the van. The phone began ringing as I slid the van door closed, and I hurried in to answer. It was Mike.

"I'm going car shopping," he said. "Want to come along?"

"You're buying a new car?"

"New, used, whichever. A car is only wheels. I thought you might like to pick the color."

"Sure. Any color as long as it's black."

"Thank you, Mrs. Ford. Okay, okay. I'll go alone."

"Good hunting."

DIGGING THROUGH reference books and price guides used up most of Thursday. When I'd gone as far as they would take me, I phoned Canterbury House.

Gordon answered.

"They're out cataloguing an estate," he said when I asked to speak to either Charlie or Rafe. "Would you like the number?"

"I don't want to bother them."

"They asked to have calls forwarded. Wait just a moment, I'll have to go to the back."

I could see Gordon in my mind's eye. He would set the phone down. He would take his characteristic two-second beat. Then the shoulders would go back, the head rise, and he would march down the length of the shop like a patrician on his way to the guillotine.

Gordon Chase has been in and out of Charlie and Rafe's lives for the past three years, which means I've known him that long. He never calls me by my name—I'm not sure he knows it. He never says more to me than is absolutely necessary, and he has never, in three years, met my eyes.

"Hell no," Charlie said when I asked him if Gordon disliked me. "He's that way with everybody."

"Except when he has to deal with a customer," Rafe said. "Then he does a takeoff on Charlie. He can do Charlie better than Charlie can."

Gordon is tall and handsome in a middle-aged way. His resonant voice and the elegance with which he wears his expensive, superbly fitted suits are totally deceptive. He's the most painfully repressed man I've ever met.

A sometime client of Canterbury House, he had offered his services on an hourly basis. Charlie and Rafe had leapt at acquiring a knowledgeable substitute without the need to carry a salaried employee, and the arrangement had endured.

I heard the scrape of the phone being picked up, then Gordon's voice said in my ear, "The number is six-two-one, then four and three zeros. I will repeat it. Six-two-one. Four. Three zeros."

He hung up without saying good-bye.

I dialed the number he had given me. A woman answered, and I asked to speak to either Mr. Harwood or Mr. Verdoni.

Two minutes passed, then Rafe said hello.

"Hi, Rafe. Am I disturbing you?"

"Not at all. What's the problem?"

"I have a box of Sam's better pieces and I thought you might be interested in having a look before I pack them for the flea market."

"If they're Sam's, we've probably seen most of it."

"Have you seen his six ivory netsukes?"

"No. What else do you have?"

"Forty-two items. No junk." I described a few of the articles. "There's one piece I can't get a fix on. Maybe you can help me. She's a carved ivory Oriental lady about five inches long, lying on a rosewood bench. She's naked, except for shoes and a disdainful expression.''

"Doctor's lady," Rafe said.

"She's a doctor's lady."

"A what?"

"At one time, in China, doctors kept these ladies on their desks so their female patients could point to where it hurt. What you've got is a doctor's lady."

"Thanks, Rafe. Can you give me an idea of what kind of price I can put on her?"

Rafe was silent a moment. Then he asked, "Are you taking all this stuff to Finney's on Friday?"

"No. I can't keep an eye on everything by myself at Finney's, and these are all small pieces. I'll take them to Beacon on Sunday. I have to sell quickly. Sam's daughter needs money to bury him."

"Cheerful thought," Rafe said. "Do me a favor, Cat. We probably won't be finished here until Sunday night. Would you set aside the doctor's lady? And the card case you mentioned. You said it was sterling?"

"Yes."

"We'll drop by Beacon early Sunday morning, on our way out here. I'd like to get a good look at those two particular pieces."

"Fine. I won't put them out till you get there."

"Thanks, Cat. See you Sunday."

# TWENTY-THREE

AT FINNEY'S the next morning I unpacked the two cartons first. Everything was sold before I finished setting up, purchased by neighboring vendors, who would double the prices for their own tables. More power to them. The pieces might sell quickly or be carried for weeks. Meanwhile, I had a fast two hundred dollars and change for Sandy.

Old Sam's space remained empty until six-thirty, when a rust-scarred pickup truck rattled in and parked beside Rena's van. It shuddered, huffed oily exhaust fumes, then sighed and relaxed for the day.

The door swung wide and a man with a wild halo of grizzled hair jumped down.

Vivid blue wraparound sunglasses rested on his nose. An unlit cigar butt protruded from the corner of his mouth. His muscular shoulders and arms strained at a splashy red and orange hibiscus-print shirt. Hairy legs emerged from his lime green shorts and ended in a pair of white boat-size athletic shoes.

It took a moment for my eyes to absorb all the splendor and focus on the face.

*"Kostas?"* I gaped incredulously.

A wide smile curved around the dead stogy. "Good morning, Catherine." He raised his right arm and swept it through the air in a gesture encompassing me, the day, the flea market, the entire universe. "And a very good morning to all. Let the games begin!"

Dropping the tailgate of his truck, he began to unload, strewing his space with rusty garden tools, wooden school desks, chrome stools with split plastic seats, half a dozen old bicycles, a stack of lawn chairs in need of rewebbing, and several boxes of crockery.

Then he set out a box of battered Harlequin paperbacks. I felt a stab of sour disappointment.

Tina would have her wedding.

Kostas spread a faded plastic shower curtain patterned with flamingoes on the pavement and emptied eight garbage bags of clothing onto it, finishing just as the first crappy chords of "Achy Breaky Heart" blasted forth.

He winced, glanced at me and grinned. He removed the cigar, flicked it with his fingers, and said in a gravelly Groucho Marx voice, "Wanna dance?"

I shook my head. "I'll wait for a waltz."

I wandered over to the mound of clothing. I had caught a glimpse of something silky-looking in a pale color and I wanted a better look at it.

It was perfect, a silk damask negligee Mae West might have worn, trimmed with enough marabou to stuff a good-size pillow. Once white, it had aged to a mellow ivory. Stains and a cigarette burn marred the front, but there was enough usable fabric in the back and sleeves to fashion a bag for Charlie and Rafe's sewing table.

I held up the robe. "How much?"

He pushed the dark glasses up onto the top of his head, worked the cigar stub back to the corner of his mouth.

"I gotta tell you, modom, it is not you." He tilted his head, removed the cigar butt, and pursed his lips. "Modom is more the grand dame type, don't we think?"

"We don't think," I said more curtly than I intended. "How much?"

He hesitated, then only his lips smiled. He hid his eyes behind the blue glasses.

"Well, naow," he drawled, "I figure fifty bucks is a fair price for all them there goose feathers. But what the hey. For you? Gimme three bucks."

I paid him and asked if Sam's space belonged to him now.

"Yes." He clamped the cigar firmly back between his teeth. "Too bad about Sam. It's a sad way to go, and I weep for the family. But life goes on."

He gestured beyond me with a jerk of his head. "You have customers," he said.

A busload of day-tour junketeers had arrived, all senior citizens, all dressed for the day in their sensible walking shoes, Bermuda shorts, color-coordinated and freshly pressed print blouses and shirts, sunglasses, and shade hats.

They do the flea market, spreading like molasses on a plate. They twitter and chatter and dawdle, the women with a firm grip on their shoulder bags, the men with their hands buried deep in their pockets.

The older flea market vendors view these golden-agers with uncharitable disdain. Disdain tinged with envy.

Born in the early thirties, married in the postwar fifties, they've passed careful lives in a defined and simpler world, the men safe in their lifelong jobs, the women protected by their husbands' dependable-as-death, regular-as-taxes paychecks.

Although it's probably not so, life appears to have dealt them only the lesser tragedies. They seem to have sailed into retirement with mortgages paid, children grown and gone, money to spend, and seemingly endless days in which to spend it.

Mike says this present generation of privileged aged is the last, and he's probably right. Job security is history. Women are no longer able to stay home and wear pretty aprons. And there's a strong possibility today's pension dollar will be tomorrow's small change.

Not knowing they're an endangered species, this bunch wandered the market in their usual jaundiced way, the women petulant, the men bored and surly.

"For Pete's sake, Edie."

Scowling under his peaked cap, the man with the football concealed under his flowery shirt tugged at his wife's thin white arm.

"We gotta get back on to the bus," he carped. "There's a storm coming an' it's coming in fast. Let's go."

"All right, Jerry. All right." Edie yanked her arm free. "Why do you always have to spoil everything?"

"What d'you mean, me spoil. You think I've got some direct line I can say rain and it rains? Take a look at the sky for Pete's sake!"

I looked. Jerry was right.

Huge hammerhead clouds scudded up from a black horizon, driven by a hurtling wind. A flock of birds wheeled and fled, crying panic, their screams lost in a thunderclap, crashing and grumbling in echo.

I ran for the plastic sheets and clamps Rena kept in the van. By the time I found them wedged under the passenger seat, the clouds had swallowed the sun and the wind was whipping up spiraling dust devils.

There was no point in unfolding the plastic sheets, they'd have been torn out of my hands. I left them and scurried out to save Rena's better pieces.

The deluge came, sheets of rain slashing horizontally. I was soaked to the skin in seconds. I tacked against the wind, back to the shelter of the van, clutching Rena's cashbox and a tall Dresden candlestick, plucking it up as it was about to blow away.

Under other circumstances, I'd have enjoyed the drama of the summer storm, the magnificent rumbling of Thor's chariot riding the clouds, the electric blue of lightning forks streaking from sky to earth. Old Mother Nature reminding us who really runs this planet.

Now, all I could envision was the havoc created by wind and water in the flea market. Encapsulated in the van, I sat drinking coffee behind the streaming windows, waiting for the Sturm und Drang to end.

Twenty minutes later the worst had passed. A lowering sky settled in, and a steady drizzle of dismal gray rain.

I climbed out of the van and looked around.

Considering the force of the wind, and apart from the litter against every obstacle, piled deep and wet, the damage in the immediate vicinity was less than I had expected.

Across the way a metal folding table had collapsed and lay amid shards of broken pottery and shattered glass. In the adjoining booth a tall bookcase had blown over, tearing through the canvas of a very large, very bad oil painting. What remained of my neighbor's heap of clothing was a sodden mass, and I was thankful I'd dredged up the damask negligee before the storm struck.

The paperbacks on Rena's tables were a write-off. A stand of brass fireplace tools had tipped and nailed down the linens, but the stuffed toys hadn't fared as well. Half had vanished, those that remained were sodden. A fallen crystal lamp had survived intact, but its silk shade had been gored by the torch a spelter Lady Liberty held aloft.

I picked up the ear of a broken teacup, but after one look at the dingy sky I said the hell with it and reached under the table for the packing crates.

Making no attempt to sort out damaged pieces, I packed quickly, emptying rainwater from bowls and cups and planters, wrapping everything in sodden newspaper, brushing my streaming hair back with ink-stained fingers and not giving a damn if my face turned black.

Piling the dripping tablecloths into a limp cardboard carton, I took down the metal tables, carried them to the van, and squished back for one of the boxes.

"Here. Give me that."

Still wearing the blue glasses, still with his dead stogie clamped in his teeth, Kostas took the box from my hands and stowed it in the van.

"Leave this." He kicked the carton into which I had dropped the paperbacks and toys. "With the kind of rent they collect, they can cart it away."

Within minutes he had everything loaded. He deposited the last box and slid the van door closed, turning to me and smiling around his cigar.

"I have hot tea," he said. "Would you like a cup?"

"Thanks, but I just want to get out of here," I said. "Thank you for all your help."

"For you?" He removed the dark glasses. With a courtly bow, he swept them as he would have a plumed hat in another era. "Any time."

I couldn't help laughing. His broad gestures should have been ludicrous, but somehow they weren't. Whatever else, Kostas had style. I started the van, and waved as I pulled away.

"Next week will be better," he called after me.


ANYONE WHO THINKS flea-marketing is fun should spend the afternoon as I did.

After I emptied the van, I set up the metal tables and wiped them down with a towel.

I carried all the crates and boxes into the kitchen, unpacked and discarded everything cracked or broken, washed and dried every salvaged item, and repacked it all.

I threw the dark blue tablecloths into the dryer—the linens had to go into the washing machine first. It was seven-thirty when I finished folding them. They would have to be ironed but not today, not by me. I had been up and running since four in the morning, fifteen hours straight. I had barely the strength to eat my nuked noodles Alfredo.

More than anything in the world I wanted a gentle, large person to come by and lift me from my chair, wash my dirty face, and tuck me into bed.

The phone shrilled and I reached for it, thinking it was Rena calling.

There was a clicking sound, then a mechanical voice launched into a recorded sales pitch for a cemetery plot.

I yanked the goddamn phone jack out of the wall and tottered down the hall to bed.

# TWENTY-FOUR

*"CAT? Where are you? Where the hell are you!"*

The words echoed down the long, black tunnel where I floated, unable to touch walls or ground.

Far ahead I could see a narrow horizontal band of shimmering light. I wriggled my fingers in an effort to propel myself toward it, aware of a terrible urgency. It seemed to be of vast importance that I reach it.

"Aw, for Christ's sake!"

I opened my eyes.

Mike stood beside my bed, fists on his hips, glowering down at me.

"Mike?" I closed my eyes, opened them again. He was still there. "What...how did you get in?"

"The front door wasn't locked," he said waspishly. "It wasn't even closed properly. The back door's wide open and the screen door isn't hooked. The kitchen's a mess, the lights are on, and the phone's been unplugged. What the hell's going on?"

I groaned and struggled to sit up. "What time is it?"

"It's ten-thirty." He folded his arms across his chest and glared at me. "I've been trying to get you since nine o'clock last night and I started dialing your goddamn number at six this morning.''

"I'm sorry." I rubbed my face, finally fully awake. "The storm yesterday was a disaster. I was wiped out."

"Storm? What storm?"

"The big thunderstorm yesterday."

"Must have bypassed us. Yesterday was sunny all day."

I groaned. "There really is no God."

"That you already knew. Come on. I'm taking you out for a long, leisurely brunch. In my new car. I'll give you ten minutes to get dressed."


THE CAR WAS WHITE. Very sleek, very sporty. I eyed it dubiously.

"Looks fast. What kind of car is it?"

"Firebird." Mike opened the passenger door. I hesitated. He limped around to the driver's side, waving a disgusted arm at me. "Don't be such a goddamn wuss. I'll put it on cruise control. That make you happy?"

"Uh." I got in, sinking into the cushioned bucket seat and fastening the seat belt. "Where are we going?"

"I thought Moishe's." Mike turned the key. The motor purred to life. "I'm in the mood for bagels and lox. Latkes with sour cream. Maybe a big hunk of their strawberry cheesecake. How does that sound to you?"

"Sinful."

"You can repent tomorrow."

Mike drove at a sedate speed, handling the car with an uncharacteristic gentleness. I relaxed enough to tell him about Old Sam and the Sebastian connection. He thought it comical.

"Space number thirty-five? The password a thirty-five-cent paperback? Thirty-five bucks a bag?" He grinned broadly. "Real cloak-and-dagger stuff. Was Sam also the undercover agent at that Sunday flea market of yours?"

"Beacon?" The thought hadn't occurred to me. "I don't think so. Not if Sebastian was hooked on his foreign intrigue scenario. There are only twenty-five spaces at Beacon."

"Would he rake in enough at Finney's to make Operation Screwing Sofia worth the effort?"

"Old Sam? I'm not sure, exactly, but I'd guess his take would be close to a thousand dollars on a good day. Maybe more."

"That much?" Mike's brows lifted. "Who took his place?"

"A man named Kostas Spiridakis."

"Has Kostas got the box of thirty-five-cent paperbacks?"

"Yes." I hesitated, but then I told Mike about Kostas and his sons. And Tina's wedding. Mike listened, frowning.

"So this Kostas had to be top man on Sebastian's

waiting list," Mike mused. "One little nudge and he climbs aboard the gravy train."

"No." My emphatic response surprised even me. "Kostas didn't strike me as that kind of man," I explained. "The kind who'd be capable of murder."

"Would you have thought he was capable of drug dealing?"

"Well, he's not actually dealing in drugs, is he?"

Mike threw me a dark glance.

I sighed. "Yeah, yeah. I know. Damn, I really liked the man."

We drove in silence for a minute or two, then Mike said, "Cat? What about your friend Rena. Did she know Sam was peddling the powder?"

"She must have. If I saw it, she saw it. She couldn't have avoided seeing. And she and Old Sam were close before he dumped her."

Mike shot me a startled glance.

"What do you mean he dumped her? Are you saying she and Sam were in it together?"

"No, no. That's not what I'm saying at all. I'm sure Rena had nothing to do with the powder. She and Old Sam had a relationship going. Sandy said she thought they might get married. They broke up, apparently, when this Sofia creature entered the picture."

"Well, well." Mike grinned at me. "And hell hath no fury like a woman scorned."

"You mean Rena?" I said. "Don't be silly."

"Why not Rena?"

"Rena beat Old Sam to death in a fit of jealous rage? I don't think so."

"Why not? The motive is classic."

"Oh, come on, Mike. Rena just isn't the type. She's a stolid, sensible kind of woman."

"And them's the worst kind. When they blow, they blow with a vengeance. No living thing survives."

I twisted around in my seat to face him more fully. "Are you serious?" I said.

Mike glanced at me. He shrugged.

"I don't know whether I'm serious or not. But think about it, Cat. Whoever snuffed Sam, it had to be someone he knew. And he sure as hell knew Rena."

"Rena was barely out of the hospital when Old Sam was killed. She wouldn't have had the strength."

"How much strength does it take to crack a man's skull with a tire iron? Particularly if he isn't expecting it?"

"What tire iron? And she didn't have a car—I had her van, remember? How would she get to Lake Echo?"

"Ever hear of rent-a-car?" Mike slowed to enter the parking lot at Moishe's and pulled into a space. "Or maybe she took a bus."

"She could have. But how would she have known Old Sam was going to Lake Echo in the first place?"

"From Sandy. Sandy was at the flea market on

Friday. Early. She could have called Rena later in the day. It's possible.''

"Hey, anything's possible. I suppose it's even possible Sandy did the dirty deed.''

Mike killed the motor. He frowned at me.

"Sandy? Sandy struck me as a very nice kid. What the hell kind of motive would she have to kill her own father?''

"Well, my goodness. Here's this innocent young thing who finds out Daddy is a baby-laxative pusher. She is totally devastated. She tries to persuade—''

"Stuff a sock in it, Cat,'' Mike interrupted dryly. He unbuckled his seat belt. "Let's go eat.''

THE LONG, LAZY BRUNCH led to a long, leisurely drive in the country. It was almost five when we returned home. Mike decided against coming in for an early dinner.

"Thanks,'' he said, "but I think I'll pass. I've already eaten too much. I've been up since five-frigging-thirty this morning. I've polluted my lungs with all that fresh air and I missed my afternoon siesta. I'm going home to bed.''

I was grateful. In spite of having slept late, I felt a bone-weariness creeping in. Finney's had taken more out of me than I had to lose.

The phone was ringing as I unlocked the door. I hurried to answer.

"Catherine? This is Rena. I'm glad I caught you. I have been trying to get you since last night but I kept getting a busy signal. I heard the storm hit Finney's pretty hard.''

"I'm sorry, Rena. I should have called. I had to dump all the paperbacks and the stuffed toys. A few pieces were cracked or broken, but it could have been a lot worse.''

"I know. Elsa lost a cheval mirror and a pair of lamps. But this is not why I have been trying to get you. I was calling to let you know you are off the hook.''

"Off the hook? What d'you mean?''

"The bakery where Frank works had a fire yesterday. It seems as if they must be closed down for a few weeks. Frank has offered to do the flea markets with me until the repairs are done with. So you are off the hook.''

"Are you sure you're well enough?''

"I am well enough to sit and sell. Frank will do the lifting and carrying.''

I felt a rush of sheer gladness. No more Finney's at five a.m. No Beacon tomorrow.

I could call Mike and ask him to come back. Have him follow me to Rena's and return her van. He'd complain, but he'd do it. Or maybe Frank could bring Rena here. She could drive the van back. And the pieces I'd set aside for Charlie and Rafe. I could explain to Rena...

It was all too complicated. And too exhausting.

"That's great, Rena.'' I said, "but I don't think I can get the van back to you tonight. Why don't I finish Beacon tomorrow and bring it over on Monday? That'll give you time to get new stock together for Finney's. You're going to need it. And it'll give you another week of recuperating."

There were several moments of silence. Then Rena said, "Are you sure you want to do this, Catherine?"

"I'm sure," I assured her. I doubt I'd have offered so freely had the next day been Finney's. "By the way, you have a new neighbor. A real comedian."

"Who?"

"A vendor named Kostas Spiridakis."

"Kostas? I don't know any Kostas."

"Remember Tina? Eight years ago? Her father."

"I don't remember him. What does he look like?"

"Wild gray hair. Big blue outer-space glasses. Big nose. A dead cigar stuck in his face. Psychedelic clothes."

"Oh, him! Zorba the Greek. Everybody knows him. It is since his wife died, two, maybe three years ago, the way he dresses, the way he behaves. He is a character, that one. He is Zorba the Greek."

"Sounds like you like him."

"He is all right."

"Well, good. He's your new neighbor at Finney's. And speaking of Finney's, tell Sandy I have a little over two hundred dollars for her."

"She found Sam's cash."

"She did? Great. Where did she find it?"

"In a stereo speaker box. There was no speaker inside, only money. Almost eighteen thousand dollars. Sandy said to tell you she would never have found it if you had not told her to check everything."

"Tell her I'll have more after tomorrow. I'm taking Old Sam's better pieces to Beacon. By the way, did she bring you the boxes of jewelry?"

"Yes."

"Anything good?"

There was a long silence. "All of it," she finally said in an oddly strained voice. "I do not understand this, Catherine. Three boxes full of very expensive jewelry."

"Maybe Old Sam had it on consignment. Charlie said he often carried good jewelry around, selling on consignment."

"Yes, yes. A piece here, a piece there. Nothing like this. One is a platinum bracelet set with graduated diamonds. Gold rings. Pins. Earrings. A pearl necklace with an emerald clasp." Rena sounded frightened. "There is so much of it, Catherine. Where did Sam get it all?"

"Who knows?" I stifled a massive yawn. "Hang on to it. Sooner or later somebody is going to claim it."

"Who?" Rena asked doubtfully. "And if nobody does?"

"Then give it to Sandy. Or you sell it for her."

There was no denying the yawn.

"Sorry, Rena," I apologized when it was over. "I need a nap. I'll come over on Monday with the van. We can talk about it then."

# TWENTY-FIVE

DRIVING THROUGH the deserted Sunday morning
streets on my way to Beacon, I found myself looking
forward to the day ahead with a degree of pleasant
anticipation.

Knowing it was the last time I would have to kick
myself out of bed before dawn, and with Old Sam's
funeral expenses covered whether I sold today or
not, I decided to relax and enjoy my final hours in
never-never land.

Unloading at Beacon, I found the other vendors
in an equally cheerful mood, their dogged optimism
buoyed by the brilliance of a perfect July day.

Friday's storm had driven away the suffocating
blanket of humidity that had hung over the city for
the past week. The early morning air was clear and
fresh, the sky a vivid midsummer blue, with here
and there a lamb's-wool puff of white cloud. It was
a God's-in-his-heaven kind of day, and it was almost
possible to believe all was right in this best of all
possible worlds.

And between tales of the storm at Finney's and
Old Sam's murder, there was plenty to gossip about.
Word of Sam's death had spread slowly through the
flea market circuit, most vendors being unaware that

the Philip K. Samson of the brief newspaper report was the Old Sam they'd known for years.

"I couldn't believe it when I heard it," Helen said, pulling a carton toward her through the open rear doors of her van. "Why would anybody want to kill Old Sam?"

"The police think it was a hitchhiker," I said.

Helen turned to face me. "Then the police are stupid," she stated flatly. "Why don't they come around and talk to us? We'd tell them a thing or six. None of us would be crazy enough to pick some joker up off the road."

"That's what his daughter said."

"And she's right. How's Rena doing?"

"Better. She'll be back next week." I dragged the last carton marked BEACON from the van. "How did you make out at Finney's?"

"The storm? I took in forty bucks before it hit and lost sixty bucks worth of stock. Between that and the rent and the license, I figure I'm in the hole about a hundred bucks for the day. It could have been worse."

"You'll make it up today. It's going to be a good day."

"From your lips to God's ears. I hope we get people. Me, if I didn't have to, I wouldn't waste a gorgeous day like this in any old flea market."

She grunted as she lifted a heavy box filled with books. "Ah, well," she said. "Come on, kiddo. Duty calls."

I followed her into the mall and began setting up.

The first box I opened contained Old Sam's treasures.

I withdrew the doctor's lady and the card case,
putting them aside for Charlie and Rafe, and set out
the Wave Crest and a pair of enameled French opera
glasses.

I'm convinced that, like dog whistles, good antiques emit an ultrasonic signal, audible only to antique dealers, pickers, and dedicated collectors.
Within seconds they were two-deep at my table.

The pieces I unwrapped never made it to the ta-
bletop. They were snatched from me either to be
held on to or passed to a neighboring hand. Resolute
fingers fastened instantly on the four Royal Doulton
Tiny's; I glanced up to see whose they were and
looked into the face of Jane Marchwood, an antique
shop owner I've known and liked for years.

"Hi, Catherine," she smiled. "How much?"

I smiled back. "Hello, Jane. Seventy-five each.
Two seventy-five if you take all four."

"I'll take them," she said, and at that moment
the man next to her bumped her arm, almost knock-
ing them out of her hands. "Hey! Be careful, will
you?" she said indignantly, turning on him.

"Sorry," he mumbled.

It was Brady, pressed against the table, watching
the pieces fly with hot, angry eyes.

His hands were empty. My fleeting thought, that
he hadn't yet learned to grab fast, was cancelled out
when I brought out the box of netsukes. He had it
before the other dealers could see what it contained.

"How much?"

"One hundred each."

I knew he wouldn't buy. At a hundred each he couldn't make any money reselling them. I continued wrapping and making change for the other dealers.

"How much if I take all six?" he demanded, leaning in closer to get my attention.

"Five hundred."

I waited a moment. He said nothing, and I turned to his neighbor, a portly man with some hairy breed of beady-eyed miniature dog tucked under his arm.

"I'm waiting for this chappie to make up his mind." He tilted his head, frowning at Brady. "Come on, luv, are you going to take them or are you not? I'd like to get a look sometime this year."

Brady slammed the box down, and the man with the dog plucked it up immediately. He emptied the box onto the table and quickly selected two of the netsukes.

"I'm a dealer," he said. "What can you do on these two?"

"Ninety. Each."

"Ninety? Come on, luv. You can do better than that."

"Sorry. Ninety. Each."

"I can't make money on that, luv."

"Then maybe you should pass."

He glared at me. I smiled back and he laughed.

"All right. All right," he capitulated. "I'll take

them at ninety and no hard feelings. One can but try, right?''

''Right.'' I bagged the netsukes, took his money, and he walked away. Charlie slipped into the space he vacated.

''Cat? You have those pieces?''

I reached under the table for the doctor's lady and the card case and handed them to Charlie. He took both, glanced at them and said *sonovabitch.*

''What's the matter?''

Charlie's yellow eye narrowed at me. ''You got these from Sam?'' he demanded.

''Yes. Why? What's the matter with them?''

''Rafe!'' Charlie called down to the far end of the table. When Rafe came, carrying a miniature ivory portrait, Charlie showed him the two pieces.

''Yes or no?'' he challenged.

Rafe nodded, frowning. He gave the portrait to Charlie. ''This one too.''

''What?'' I looked at their set faces. ''What do you mean, this one too?''

''Sorry, Cat.'' Rafe's smile flicked on and off. ''These are pieces we sold to Léli.''

Charlie picked up the remaining netsukes. ''These too,'' he said.

''Have you talked to her since Charlie and I tried to see her last Saturday?''

''Haven't had the chance. We've been tied up with this estate thing all week.''

Rafe looked up into Charlie's stormy face. ''I think we should try again tomorrow.''

"Bloody right," Charlie said angrily. "And forget the try crap. We're going to see her if I have to go up the front and down the back of little chiquita Juanita to do it."

He turned to me. "We'd like to take these three pieces with us," he said. "How much are you asking?"

"Take them." I handed Charlie a bag. "If you decide to buy you can pay Rena."

"Good enough. Thanks, Cat. We'll be in touch."

Brady watched them leave, his face full of the sort of hypnoid fascination that Charlie and Rafe, taken together, seem to inspire in strangers. He felt my eyes on him and turned back to me, holding out a French cloisonn snuff bottle.

"How much?" he asked.

"Sixty-five."

He turned the bottle in his hand several times, set it down and looked at me with an expression of such hostility that I felt my scalp prickle.

"I'll think about it," he gritted, and walked away.

I watched him go, astonished. Why so snarky? The bottle was old and lovely. At sixty-five it was a bargain.

Five minutes later I sold it, together with an enamel needle case and a Staffordshire patch box, to a dealer who made more money renting to film companies than he ever did selling from his shop.

And that was my last sale of the day.

By nine-thirty, with the exception of the habitués

who have nothing better to do and never buy, the mall was empty.

At eleven, the La Cachette brunch crowd arrived, ate, dawdled briefly, and departed. Deli customers, carrying bags of milk and bread, meandered through the aisles on their way to the exits. Vendors left their booths untended and drifted from one table to the next, gossiping and complaining.

"I haven't even broken the ice," Helen said glumly. "Not one sale. The way I figure, between the storm at Finney's and today, counting rent and gas and everything else, it's cost me a couple of hundred bucks to work my behind off. I'd have done better sitting on it at home."

"It's too nice a day," Mark, the clock man, said, shrugging. "They're all out in their backyards getting sunburnt."

"*He* screwed up." Bill jabbed a thumb at the ceiling. "This was the day we were supposed to get on Friday at Finney's. If we'd of got Friday's weather today, like we were supposed to, they'd all be here."

At noon I phoned Mike and told him I'd been sprung, Rena and Frank were taking over. I asked if he'd drive with me to Rena's in the morning to return her van.

"You bet your boots," he said. "I've got a nine-thirty cardiologist appointment but that shouldn't take long. I'll be at your place before noon."

At two-thirty, by common consent, the vendors declared the day a disaster and we all began packing. I was bent over a carton when I heard a vaguely familiar voice complaining to the vendor who had taken over Old Sam's spot directly across from me.

"You can't be closing. We just got here."

I straightened up from the carton I was packing. It was the lace-tablecloth woman and her unpleasant mother, wearing identical outraged expressions.

"It isn't even three o'clock." The older woman's voice was just as querulous as her daughter's. "You can't be closing."

"It's been a long day, ma'am." The vendor, a small man with a bald, mottled pate, bright blue eyes and badly fitted false teeth, spoke mildly. "We've been here since seven o'clock this morning."

"Seven?" The woman picked up a pressed-glass candy dish. "Nobody told me you open at seven."

"Would you have been here if they had?" he asked.

"At seven? Don't be ridiculous." She gestured with the candy dish. "How much do you want for this?"

"Nine fifty, ma'am. It's marked on the lid."

"That's too much. I'll give you five dollars for it."

"I'm sorry. Nine dollars is the best I'll do."

"That's only fifty cents off. What kind of a bargain is that? This is supposed to be a flea market."

"Sorry. Nine dollars."

The woman flicked the candy dish with her finger. It gave back the dull thud of pressed glass.

"It isn't even crystal," she snapped. "It certainly isn't worth nine dollars. I'll take it for five-fifty."

The little man eyed her expressionlessly.

He reached across the table, removed the cover from the candy dish and with great deliberation opened his fingers and let it fall to the floor.

The glass shattered on the terrazzo, scattering shards and splinters over her shoes and into the surrounding aisle.

"There you are, ma'am. Now you can have it for five."

The woman gaped wordlessly at him. She let the bottom of the candy dish drop to the table. Dragging her wide-eyed mother with her, she scuttled away.

He watched them go, a bemused expression on his face. Catching my eye on him, he said, "Always wanted to do that."

He picked up the bottom of the candy dish, wrapped it in newspaper, and packed it, nodding across the aisle at me.

"Felt as good as I thought it would, too." he said.

# TWENTY-SIX

A FAMILY of sparrows squabbling in the oak tree outside my bedroom window wakened me at seven-thirty.

I stretched luxuriously, feeling like a kid on the first day of summer vacation. No more pencils, no more books, no more teacher's cross-eyed looks.

I got out of bed without my usual creaking and groaning, showered for five lavishly steamy minutes, donned a pair of cutoff shorts and a T-shirt, and waltzed to the kitchen to put coffee on to perk.

Then I called Rena.

"We'll be there around noon," I told her. "Is that all right with you?"

"Fine. I'll be here. How did it go yesterday?"

"Terrible. I sold most of Old Sam's pieces to dealers in the morning. After that, nothing. The place was dead. We packed up early."

"I thought it would be quiet. It was just too nice a day. How did the others do?"

"About the same as I did with your stuff. Not a single sale all day. Sorry, Rena."

"It was not your fault, Catherine. That's the way it goes sometimes."

"True. Rena? If you see Sandy, tell her I have close to a thousand dollars for her."

"I'll tell her."

"See you later then."

Still basking in a holiday feeling, I decided to make the kind of breakfast I'd been missing for the past three weeks. I diced ham, chopped shallots, whisked two eggs, and dumped everything into hot butter in my favorite old cast-iron frying pan.

I was splitting an English muffin when the phone rang.

"Hello, Cat. It's me," Charlie said. His voice sounded hollow and distant. "Have you been listening to the news?"

"No. I haven't even read the morning paper."

"It's not in the paper. Yet." Charlie coughed, clearing his throat. "Cat," he said huskily, "Léli's dead."

*"What?"*

"She's dead. She was burned...they were burned alive. Léli and that little Juanita woman."

"Burned...oh my God, Charlie. When?"

"Early this morning. The fire trucks were packing up when Rafe and I got there."

Charlie coughed again. "Sorry, Cat, I'm still in shock. One of the firemen told us it must have started around four in the morning. He said by the time they found the damn house... He said the way that place is laid out is criminal. You remember, Cat. We got lost. He said there was no way they could get into the house. All they could do was keep pumping water. Put out the fire and keep it from spreading to the other houses."

"Are they sure Léli and Juanita were there? Maybe—"

"They're sure. They found them upstairs in their beds." Charlie coughed, hacking in my ear. "Sorry, Cat. I can still taste the ashes. I can still smell the smoke."

So, I suddenly realized, could I. I turned my head.

A cloud of dark smoke was billowing up from the frying pan and curling around the range hood.

I dropped the phone and ran, snatching up a towel at the sink. I swept the charred pan off the element. It skittered across the stove's slick porcelain surface and crashed to the floor, inches from my bare feet. I leaped aside, cursing, switched off the glowing element and returned to the phone.

"Charlie? You still there?"

"I'm still here. Jesus Christ, Cat, what happened? It sounded like the roof was falling in. Are you all right?"

"I'm all right, Charlie dammit. I just cremated my breakfast," I said crossly, and was instantly horrified. Why couldn't I have just said *ruined?*

Fortunately, it flew over Charlie's head.

"Cat, would you tell Rena we're interested in buying the three pieces we took? If she can give us an idea of how much she wants for them?"

"Rena's never seen them." I said. "Why don't you offer the same deal you had with Léli? A third of what you can sell them for?"

"Fair enough. If she agrees, we'll send her a check."

"I'll tell her. Charlie? I'm so sorry about Léli."

"I know. Damn it, the world can't afford to lose people like Léli. Why is it the— Sorry, Cat. Customers."

He hung up.

I threw open the door to air out the kitchen and cleaned up the mess on the floor, then carried my coffee out onto the patio. I sat in the oak tree's shade and tried hard not to think of Léli and death, of the callous randomness of life, and the unfairness of it, of how so much is given to some while from others all is taken away.

And of the futility of asking why.

The only antidote to such gloom-and-doom introspection, for me, has always been physical activity. I had two pieces to refinish for Charlie, and the day was ideal for stripping. Low humidity, with a gentle breeze and a cloudless sky.

I carried the sewing table and the commode up from the basement and went back down for steel wool, spatulas, rags, and stripper.

Lifting the gallon container of stripper from the shelf, I miscalculated its weight and the large can slipped from my fingers. It dropped with a thud to the work bench below and the screw-on cap, which I must have replaced carelessly, flew off. The viscous lye-based liquid spurted out spewing me from below my breasts to my bare feet. Within seconds, my skin was on fire.

Whimpering, I set the container upright and raced for the stairs, peeling off my shirt as I ran. I jumped into the bathtub and turned the shower on full force. Standing under the cold stream, I removed my shorts and soaped my searing abdomen, legs, and feet.

When I had toweled dry and greased myself liberally with sunburn ointment, I searched my closet for something that would be less abrasive to my damaged areas than denim cutoffs and canvas sneakers.

I found a full-skirted cotton sundress and a pair of thongs. I cleaned up the basement and brought my tools upstairs. There was no point in beginning the stripping process at this late hour, so I removed the ornate brass hinges and drawer pulls from the dwarf commode, took them to the kitchen sink, and cleaned them, a job I detest.

Mike arrived as I was finishing. He sniffed the air.

"What's that stink?" he said.

"Brass cleaner. I don't like it either."

"You're wearing a dress." He eyed me with raised brows. "You never wear a dress. What's the occasion?"

"No occasion. I spilled—"

"What's the matter with your feet? They're all red."

"I spilled stripper on them."

"You should be more careful. Come on. Let's go. Let's get this over with."

"Yeah. Sure. Thanks for the sympathy," I mumbled, and followed him out of the house.

# TWENTY-SEVEN

RENA, LOOKING and sounding almost like her old self, met me at the door.

"Come in," she said. "I made fresh coffee."

"Thanks, Rena. I'll have to check with Mike."

I gestured toward Mike leaning against his car, his arms folded across his chest, a cigarette between his fingers.

"I'll ask him." Rena pulled the door shut behind her and followed me to the curb.

They took an instant dislike to each other.

Rena gave him her low-wattage vendor's smile. "Would you like to come in for coffee?"

Mike let the cigarette fall to the ground and pushed his hands into his trouser pockets.

"Thank you, Rena," he said with exquisite politeness. "Another time, perhaps. I'm afraid I'm a little pressed for time today."

"Of course." Rena's smile was fixed. "I appreciate your help. Thank you."

"You're entirely welcome." Mike turned a bland face to me. "I don't want to rush you, Cat..."

I followed Rena back to her front door, gave her the keys to her van, her cashbox, and the envelope containing Sandy's money.

As I was telling her about Charlie's offer on the three pieces he and Rafe had taken, Frank Czerny came downstairs.

He was barefoot and wearing only shorts. His chest, his forearms, his face, and his glasses were speckled with light blue paint. The color matched his pale eyes.

"Good morning, Mrs. Wilde." A smile flickered and was gone. He excused himself from a handshake by turning up a paint-smeared palm. "I'm painting the kitchen."

"How is Lucie?"

"Fine, thank you. She's taken Brandon to the doctor. He has an ear infection."

"I'm sorry to hear it. Say hello for me, will you?"

"I will." His eyes shifted to Rena. "Give me the keys. I'll put the van in the garage."

Rena handed him the keys and he walked away, nodding to Mike as he passed.

Mike watched him go, then limped around his car, hitched himself into the driver's seat, started the engine and sat drumming his fingers on the steering wheel.

"Tell Charlie the offer is fine," Rena said. "I am sure Sandy will agree." She hesitated, grasped my hand, shook it awkwardly, and let it drop. "I don't know how to thank you, Catherine."

"Don't try. You're welcome, Rena. Any time."

But not soon.

I hurried down the path to Mike's car, clambered into the passenger seat, slammed the door, fastened the seat belt—and turned on him.

"What was that all about? You didn't tell me you were pressed for time."

"I'm not," Mike grunted. He pulled away from the curb and started down the street at a reasonable speed. "I just didn't want her damn coffee. I didn't like the woman."

"That was obvious. Why not?"

"I don't like women who don't wear lipstick."

"What?"

"I don't like naked faces on women."

"What are you talking about?"

"Visual pollution. I'm talking about visual polluters. Littering. Dog poop. Graffiti. Junkyards."

"What on earth do dog poop and junkyards have to do with Rena and lipstick?"

"Everything. There's enough ugliness in the world without people deliberately adding to it. Unsightliness is an imposition on the observer. Like teenagers with dirty hair and rings in their snotty noses. Like men with stubble on their chins. Like your friend there. That hatchet haircut. The scraggy eyebrows. The putty lips. The woman's an offense to the eye."

"She's the way God made her, for Pete's sake."

"God only provided the basics. Women have an

obligation to beautify themselves. And the planet.''

"Oh, brother.''

"Come on, Cat,'' Mike shot me a sideways glance. "She didn't like me either.''

No point in denying it. I let the subject drop.

"What did the cardiologist say?'' I asked.

"He prescribed a new pill. Big deal.''

"But you will take them.''

"I'm thinking about it.''

"What's there to think about? He wouldn't prescribe them if you didn't need them. Maybe you should put some thought into quitting smoking instead.''

"Back off, Cat, godammit.''

We drove a couple of blocks in silence.

"Want to stop for coffee or something?'' Mike asked while we waited for a red light to change.

"Thanks, but I'd like to go straight home. I have two pieces to strip for Charlie and Rafe, and today's a perfect day to do it.''

"Whatever you say,'' Mike said stiffly.

The light switched to green. Mike tramped down on the accelerator and we shot up the ramp and onto the freeway.

I looked across at his set jaw and thought, Darn you, Mike. You can be a such an obstinate old prick-lepuss sometimes.

And if anything should happen to you this world would be a darker and a lonelier place.

"Tell you what," I said. "Give me a couple of hours. I'll strip the two pieces. Then we'll go to that new place where you eat on the deck, right over the lake. There's to be a full moon tonight. It'll be a beautiful evening to dine under the stars."

Mike flashed me a genuine smile. "Sounds good to me."

"Let's get all dressed up like real people for a change. Let's celebrate."

"What are we celebrating?"

"How about just being alive?" I said.

And told him all about Léli.

# TWENTY-EIGHT

MIKE DROPPED ME at home and drove off to have his new prescription filled, get a haircut, and change his clothes, promising to return in a couple of hours.

I changed into shorts and T-shirt and carried the commode, the sewing table, and all my paraphernalia out to the patio at the rear of the house.

Setting the commode's drawers aside, I placed it and the table on old newspaper, poured the stripper fluid into a deep, porcelain-lined clay bowl.

With a broad brush, I slathered stripper on the surfaces of both pieces and sat back in a lawn chair to wait till it bubbled.

A flash of red caught the corner of my eye and I tilted my head. Perched on the lowest branch of the oak tree was a cardinal, preening his wings.

My sudden movement startled him into stillness. With a swift, beady-eyed glance he was off and soaring, scarlet in the limpid sky.

I heaved a sigh of contentment. No more flea-marketing. I ignored a small twinge of guilt at the thought that it was misfortune that had made Frank available. Available, and willing. I remembered Lucie telling me Frank would do anything for Rena.

I sat up abruptly.

Anything?

*Like driving Rena to Lake Echo?*

Vivid imagery spilled into my mind. The muscularity of Frank's arms and shoulders. Old Sam, disarmed by a pair of familiar faces. The brutal killing. How many blows would it take to beat a man to death? The cold-blooded way his body had been left like road kill in a ditch. An odious, tandem drive back to town.

Melodrama. Women don't murder men who dump them.

They don't? What of Jean Harris and that Scarsdale diet doctor? Strange, I remember her name. Not his.

Too agitated to remain seated, I pulled on a pair of rubber gloves, snatched up the spatula, and began scraping at the gummy varnish raised by the stripper.

How well do I know Rena, really?

Eight years ago, companionably enough, we had shared flea market time and space. We had exchanged life histories, empathized over the loss of our children, her Stepan to a lifetime of childhood, my Laurie to eternity. But beyond that we had never delved beneath the surface of what was, after all, maybe not so much friendship as useful acquaintanceship.

Do I really know what makes Rena tick? Do I believe her capable of plotting and carrying out the killing of Old Sam? Could I say, unequivocally, that she isn't?

Dammit, Mike. You've poisoned my mind.

"Nice little place you've got here."

I swung around, startled.

Old Sam's pet peeve, the vendor named Brady, stood in the kitchen doorway, leaning nonchalantly against the doorframe, his hands tucked into the rear pockets of his jeans. His unbuttoned olive camouflage-print vest hung open, revealing a hairless chest.

"How did you get into the house?" I demanded.

"I opened the door and walked in." One shoulder lifted and fell. "It wasn't locked."

"I didn't hear the doorbell."

"Maybe because I didn't ring it."

I felt a small flutter of apprehension and covered it by asking, more sharply than I intended, "What are you doing here? What do you want?"

He ignored me and stepped out onto the patio. His eyes drifted across the expanse of grass beyond the oak tree to the high cedar hedge surrounding the yard.

"Nice privacy," he said, and added in the same amiable tone, "I want the rest of the stuff."

"What stuff?"

He turned his gaze back on me, his face expressionless.

"Go on," he said. "Get it."

"Get *what?* What are you talking about?"

"Don't horseshit me, lady," he said. "You were selling some of it yesterday. Those netsukes were mine. The snuff bottle you tried to sell me was mine."

There was menace in his uncadenced tone. With his head, thrust forward and his hair skinned back into a lank ponytail, he was somehow birdlike. A vulture. I backed away·to put the patio work bench between us.

"I'm sorry," I reached for conciliatory words. "You're mistaken. It's understandable. Netsukes can look a lot alike. But the ones I sold yesterday belonged to Old Sam."

"Like hell they did. He stole them from me."

"He what?" I stifled a nervous impulse to giggle at the shift from menace to petulance in Brady's voice. "How could he steal them from you?"

"He followed me," Brady glared. His eyes narrowed. "*God damn.* You were in on it with him."

"In on what?" I snapped, exasperation momentarily overcoming my growing sense of fear. "I don't know what you're talking about."

"Sure you do. That's why he gave you the stuff."

"He didn't give me anything," I protested. "Look, I went to Old Sam's apartment last week. *After* he was killed. I picked up three boxes of stuff. All the pieces I sold at Beacon yesterday came out one of them."

"You're lying." Brady said flatly. "I went to his

place last week myself. None of his keys fit the door. How did you get in if I couldn't?''

''I went with his…''

The words died in my throat. There was only one way Brady could have come into possession of Old Sam's keys.

We stared mutely at one another.

Brady blinked first, a lazy lowering and raising of the lids that sent a chill up my spine. He withdrew his hand from his vest pocket. His fingers were curled around a gun.

It was small. It was black. And it was pointed at me.

For the first time I regretted the isolation provided by the dense cedar hedge. We were alone. I pressed my hands flat on the bench to still their trembling.

''Is that thing real?'' My voice cracked on the last word.

The gun veered away from me. He extended his arm, sighting along it. I turned to see what he was aiming at.

A plump, bushy-tailed gray squirrel twitched on a limb of the oak tree, chewing his fingernails and watching us with bright, nervous eyes. I heard a popping sound, no louder than an inflated paper bag bursting, and the squirrel plummeted to the ground.

I looked back at Brady, horrified.

''What did you do that for?'' I said shakily.

''I was making a point.'' Brady switched his

happy-face smile on full strength. It was obscene. "I wasn't ready when Sam hijacked me. I am now, okay? Okay. There were three boxes full of jewelry. I want them back and I want them now. Go get them. And I mean now."

"I don't have them."

I heard the slam of a car door. Mike.

There was no reaction from Brady. He had either not heard or assumed the noise came from the street.

"You're lying again," he said calmly.

He raised the gun and I found myself staring into the small, round black hole at the end of the barrel. He was less than five feet from me. He couldn't miss.

"Hey! I'm back!" Mike's voice sang out from inside the house. "I skipped the haircut. Too many customers. Cat? Where are you?"

Brady went rigid. He glared at me, outraged.

Thoughts flashed through my head.

Mike will guess where I am. He'll be at the kitchen door in seconds. This lunatic won't kill me, not until he gets his hands on the jewelry.

But he *will* shoot Mike.

*No.*

Before Brady could turn toward the house, I snatched up the clay bowl and threw the stripper fluid in his face.

His eyes flew wide. For a heartbeat he glared disbelief and rage, then the viscous liquid smeared away his features and he howled, a shriek of pain

so primal my skin shrank in a surge of purely ata-
vistic fear.

He fell to the ground, clawing at his eyes, and
curled into a fetal position, screaming on every ex-
haled breath. I stared down at him, frozen.

"Cat! What the hell!"

Mike was suddenly beside me, clutching my arm.

"Call the police!" I shouted above the ululating
horror writhing at my feet. *"Call the police!"*

Regaining control of my limbs, I ran for the garden hose coiled over a water tap projecting from the
side of the house. In my haste I knocked half the
hose off the tap, and it fell to the ground in a tangle
of green plastic loops. I scrabbled for the nozzle end,
turned the tap on full, and hurried back to Brady,
dragging the hose after me and adjusting the jetting
water to a spray as I ran.

His screams were hoarser now. His body jerked
sideways in an odd crablike movement, his heels
slipping and scraping on the patio stones as he tried
to propel himself away from the pain inflicted by
his jeans. From the waistband almost to his knees
the denim was stained dark with stripper fluid and
plastered against his groin and thighs.

I dropped the hose and knelt beside him, shivering
as I fumbled at the metal button on the waistband.
My fingers refused to cooperate.

"They're on their way." Mike came running
from the house and stopped dead in his tracks when

he saw me. "For Christ's sake...Cat, what in hell are you doing?"

"We've got to get his jeans off," I panted up at him. "The stripper'll burn the skin right off his plumbing."

Mike winced. "Jesus," he said, and knelt beside me. "Move over, Cat. Let me try."

I backed off and picked up the hose, spraying Brady's chest and head while Mike fought his spastic resistance. Tugging and grunting, he managed to yank the jeans down to Brady's boots and I turned the cold spray on the bare, inflamed skin of Brady's abdomen and crotch. His ragged screams dissolved into a high-pitched, agonized keening.

Mike struggled to his feet, stripping off his wet seer-sucker jacket. He turned to lay it on the patio table and saw two policeman appear at the corner of the house.

"The cops," he said, and called to them. "Over here!"

Two blue-shirted policeman hurried forward. The older, heavier man I recognized as Quinn, the policeman who'd taken the call when my house was trashed by teenagers a couple of years back.

He eyed me, frowning.

"Mrs. Wilde? It is Mrs. Wilde, isn't it?" I nodded and his glance slid from the naked Brady, to Mike, to me. "What the hell is going on here?" he said.

"You have to get him to a hospital." I thrust the hose into Quinn's hand. "Keep spraying him. Try to get his hands away from his face. I'll get a towel."

I ran into the house, snatched a bath towel from the hall closet, and raced back outside.

"Here," I handed the towel to Quinn. "Wrap this around him. Get him to the hospital as quickly as you can."

Quinn took the towel, dropping the hose.

"What's the matter with him?" he asked.

"I threw stripper fluid at him," I explained. "It's very caustic. I think a lot of it went in his eyes."

"Stripper fluid?" Quinn squinted. "Now why would you be doing that?"

"He shot a squirrel." I was suddenly aware of Brady's empty hands. "There's a gun around here somewhere. He must have dropped it."

"He shot a squirrel," Quinn stated carefully. "You threw stripper in his face because he shot a squirrel."

"Cat..." Mike shook his head at me. "You're not making sense. Who is this guy anyway?"

"He killed Old Sam, Mike. I thought he was going to kill you." I turned to Quinn. "Look, it's a long story. I'll tell you later. Please, can you get him to the hospital now?"

Quinn handed the towel to the younger officer.

"Wrap him up," he said, and narrowed his eyes at me. "We can settle this later. We'll get him to the hospital fast and come back. Wait here for us."

He bent over Brady, lifted him by the waist, slung

him fireman-style over his shoulder with swift, practiced ease, and trod heavily away, followed by his
partner.

We trailed them to the front of the house.

Quinn deposited the moaning Brady on the back-
seat of the police cruiser, handling him with sur-
prising gentleness. He slammed the door shut and
climbed into the passenger seat beside the younger
man.

"Wait for us," he said sternly.

We watched the cruiser back down the driveway
and pull away into the street. A moment later the
siren began to wail.

# TWENTY-NINE

"THE STRIPPER burned his eyes," Mike said. "He's blind. He'll never see again."

We were seated at the patio table, Charlie and Rafe, Mike and I, under the oak tree, eating the Greek takeout Rafe and Charlie had picked up on their way to collect the sewing table and demilune commode.

It was Saturday, the final day of what had been a disturbed and depressing week.

On Tuesday the four of us went together to Léli's funeral, held in a nondenominational graveyard chapel too cramped to accommodate the mourners. We stood outside throughout the brief ceremony, then walked with the others up the hill to the gravesite beside Aaron's.

It was a strange crowd.

Some of the mourners were white-haired and well-dressed, people Charlie recognized from Aaron's funeral. There were young men and women, their skin ranging from ivory to purest ebony, many of them accompanied by uncharacteristically subdued children. There was a group of the aged and infirm, some with canes, three in wheelchairs. Middle-aged men in dated suits stood with faded women carrying worn, plastic purses. A small band of teen-agers replete with dreadlocks and nose rings huddled together, quietly defensive.

And Al Rosen, a homicide detective Mike knew fairly well.

He was a thickset man of average height, some-where in his forties, dressed in a dark suit, a black yarmulke pinned to his thick, graying hair. His face was sallow, with full lips set in the shadow of a beard he must have to shave twice a day. Behind his heavy-rimmed glasses were eyes as sharp and alert as a hawk's.

"They're from the clinics." His gaze skimmed the crowd. "Some of them work at one or another of the downtown clinics. Most of them are patients. They all knew Léli."

"Did you know her?" Charlie asked.

"Léli?" Rosen swept Charlie with a practiced eye. "I've known Léli since her Jewish General days. She was one very special lady."

"We thought she was too," Charlie said.

"Is Brady yours, Al?" Mike asked.

Rosen nodded. "He's mine," he said.

"How's it going?"

Rosen hesitated, then said, "We'll have it wrapped up before the weekend."

"Do you think you could let me know? This isn't idle curiosity, Al. These people were directly in-volved."

Rosen's eyes traveled from Charlie to me, lingered on Rafe, and returned to Mike.

"Sure. I'll be in touch, Mike."

He walked away down the line of parked cars bending to unlock the door of a dark blue sedan. With a nod to us he got in a drove away.

Throughout the week we all saw a good deal of Al Rosen.

I told my story, first to Quinn, then to Rosen and his partner, Ivan Royko, a quiet younger man with sandy hair, a receding chin, and clever eyes, who was meticulously picking up the threads of Old Sam's murder and weaving them into the deaths of Léli and Juanita Santos.

He questioned Sandy, Mike, and me regarding Old Sam's last day at Finney's, seeming undiscouraged by how little detail we were able to provide.

Charlie and Rafe were called on to identify Léli's possessions found in Brady's apartment. The insurance files identified Léli's jewelery.

Rena told Rosen all she knew about Brady, which turned out to be not much.

We learned Brady's first name was Paul.

Paul Brady. Age thirty-six. At seventeen, convicted of car theft and placed on probation. At twenty-six, two years in prison for breaking and entering.

He had subsequently shacked up with a sixteen-year-old and fathered two children by her. She had walked out on him after filing repeated charges of abuse, taking the two little girls with her.

AT WEEK'S END Rosen called Mike, as good as his word. Mike had spent the better part of the day with Rosen and Royko.

"I'll give it to you the way I got it," he said, "the way the police put it together."

He pulled a small chunk of barbecued lamb free of the souvlaki stick, dipped it in tzatziki sauce, and popped it into his mouth, holding up a finger until he finished chewing.

"Royko located Brady's common-law wife through a women's shelter group. She's living in the east end, working as a supermarket cashier. She told Royko that Brady used to break into houses and steal stuff to sell at flea markets. Which is where he met Rena."

"He fooled Rena," I said. "He told her he'd lost his job. He said he had a wife and kids. You can't blame Rena."

"I'm not blaming her. He fooled a lot of people."

"She thought he was a lovely young man."

"Rena's lucky," Mike snorted. "Juanita Santos thought he was a lovely young man and she's dead."

"How did Juanita enter the picture?" Charlie asked.

"Brady met her at one of Léli's clinics. She was

working as a nurse's aide-cum-scullery maid. Brady was the clinic's maintenance man, a euphemism for sweeping floors and hauling garbage. Actually, he wasn't there long. The director of the clinic suspected him of dipping into the drug cabinet and fired him after a month.''

Mike swept aside a wasp hovering over his plate.

''Al got the story from a woman named Rosalia Torres, Juanita's friend. Rosalia detested Brady. She thought he was an evil man. She said she tried to warn Juanita, but Juanita wasn't listening. *Se apoderó de su alma,* is the way Rosalia put it.''

''He seized? Took possession?'' Rafe translated. ''He took possession of her soul?''

''Exactly.'' Mike nodded and continued.

''When Léli broke her hip and needed live-in help,'' he went on, ''she hired Juanita, borrowed her, more or less, from the clinic. With Juanita installed, Brady had access to Léli's house, and he began looting the place.''

''Léli didn't know what was happening?'' Rafe asked.

''Léli was confined to her bed. Her bedroom was the only room found still completely furnished after the fire. Léli probably never saw Brady.''

''Did he sell her furniture?'' Charlie asked. ''The Majorelle turned up, but what about the rest? I know she had a Biedermeier secretaire and a pair of Victorian armchairs. She bought them from us. Did the firemen find them?''

Mike shook his head.

"A sofa, a dining room table, badly charred. That's all there was downstairs. He was systematically cleaning the place out. He'd have had it down to bare walls if Sam hadn't moved in on him. Sam followed him to Léli's, found out what was going on, and demanded part of the action."

"It bugged Old Sam," I said. "He couldn't figure out where Brady was getting all the great stuff. And you know what? I'm the one who suggested he follow Brady. But I never dreamed he'd actually do it."

Charlie shook his head sadly. "Poor old Sam," he said. "I always knew he was a little bit bent. I never thought he was an honest-to-God crook."

"Sam wasn't a crook," Mike said. "He was just a small-time hustler with an eye out for any pair of coattails he could hitch a ride on. His problem was he never learned there are cages you don't rattle."

Mike pushed his plate aside and lit a cigarette. He inhaled deeply, blew out a stream of smoke, and settled back into his lawn chair.

"Brady had Juanita call Sam," Mike resumed. "She set him up with the phony Lake Echo estate sale. Brady met Sam there, killed him, and drove Sam's van back to town."

"Who drove Brady's van back? Juanita?" Charlie asked.

Mike shook his head.

"Royko doesn't believe so. He thinks either Brady took a bus back to Lake Echo to get his van, or he told Juanita he'd had car trouble and she drove him up. He is convinced Juanita never knew Brady killed Sam."

"Why not? She went along with robbing Léli."

"I'll get to that," Mike said. He looked around for an ashtray. I pushed a saucer across the table toward him. Somewhat sheepishly, he flicked the ash from his cigarette into it.

"So now we come to last Sunday at Beacon," he said. "Brady saw Léli's things on Cat's table, the pieces Sam had blackmailed out of him. While he was standing and sweating, Charlie and Rafe came along. They recognized the pieces they had sold to Léli. He heard them say they were going to see Léli first thing Monday morning."

"Over Juanita's dead body if need be. Or words to that effect." Charlie said. "My goodness gracious. That really must have put the wind up old Brady."

"You bet your boots it did," Mike said grimly. "He went to Léli's in the middle of the night, Sunday night, and shot both of them, Léli and Juanita, in their sleep. Then he set fire to the house."

We were silent a moment. Then Rafe asked, "Why did he kill Juanita? I can understand why he must have seen a need to dispense with Léli. We were going to be asking her a lot of embarrassing questions. But why kill Juanita?"

Mike dropped his cigarette butt on the patio stone and ground it with his foot.

"This is the way Royko, who is Catholic, reads it, and it's why he thinks Juanita knew nothing of Sam's murder. Juanita was a devout believer, the kind of Catholic who takes every dogma as absolute truth. She may have been able to justify the thieving. Dr. Steinhauer was rich, she could always buy more. Or maybe she thought Brady was worth a few eons in purgatory. Who knows? But killing is a completely other bucket of blood. For murder, you fry in hell for all eternity. Both Royko and Rosen believe Juanita balked. Or it could be Brady was afraid she'd be overcome with an attack of conscience somewhere down the line. With the Léli thing blown away, he no longer had any use for her anyway."

Mike pulled a cigarette halfway out of the package. He pushed it back and reached for a black olive.

"Now we come to the bottom line," he said.

He chewed, grimaced, spat the olive pit into his hand, and dropped it into the saucer.

"Other than having possession of Sam's keys, Rosen isn't convinced they can build a solid case against Brady for Sam's murder. But they have him nailed for Léli and Juanita."

Mike held up his left index finger.

"First, the gun. It was Léli's, registered to her. The bullets that killed Léli, Juanita, and the squirrel are a match."

He raised his middle finger. "Second, everything

found and identified by Charlie and Rafe as belonging to Léli.''

He extended his thumb, a smile on his face.

''Third and best. A witness who puts Brady in Léli's house on Sunday night, minutes before the fire started.''

''Where did they dig up a witness?'' Charlie asked. ''Not on that street.''

''On that street.'' Mike nodded. ''Royko found him. A freelance writer named Chris Lombardy. He does most of his writing after midnight, and he'd seen Brady often during the past couple of months, carrying furniture and cartons out of Léli's house. He didn't know Léli and figured it wasn't any of his business. He was working Sunday night and stood up from his computer to stretch. He looked out the window and saw Brady hurry out of Léli's house and drive away. A few minutes later he saw flames in the downstairs bay window of the house and called the fire department.''

Charlie said, ''So there actually are real people living in those houses? When Cat and I were there we didn't even see a curtain twitch.''

''Which was probably why Brady got away with as much as he did,'' Mike said. ''No nosy neighbors.''

I thought of the high cedar hedge screening me from my neighbors and the small black gun in Brady's hand.

''You know what's frightening?'' I said. ''That

there are people like Brady around who are ready to kill for a few thousand dollars.''

"What few thousand dollars?" Mike said.

"How much would he have made on Léli's things? He sold the Majorelle for forty dollars.''

"A lot more than a few thousand, Cat. Aaron's collection was insured for a hundred thousand, Léli's jewelry for half a million. Rosen found the policies in a box of papers Brady had taken from Léli's house. Brady may have goofed on the Majorelle, but he knew the value of the Judaica and the jewelry, and it added up to a hell of a lot more than a few thousand. And that doesn't include Léli's collection of small treasures. Not to mention the paintings and furniture and everything else.''

Rafe shook his head thoughtfully. "It was more than the money he was after, Mike," he said. "It was the having.''

"What do you mean," Mike frowned, "the having?"

"Having the really fine, old pieces." Rafe shifted in his chair. "And everybody knowing you have them.''

"That's worth killing for?"

Rafe smiled his half-smile and said, "There are people I know who might think so.''

"Come on, Rafe. Who?"

Rafe shrugged. "Dealers. Collectors. Investors. They may not do it, but you can bet they've thought about it once or twice.''

"You can't be serious," Mike said.

"Antiques can be an obsession, Mike. I've seen murderous fights between dealers over a choice piece. And not because of the money they might make selling it."

"You're saying Brady killed because he was obsessed?"

"No," Charlie intervened, "of course not. Brady killed to save his sorry ass. Sam not only had him by the balls, he also had the jewelry. And we were going to talk to Léli. But what Rafe says is true. There's prestige involved."

"Prestige?" Mike snorted. "What the hell kind of prestige is there in a flea market?"

"Precisely," Charlie said, nodding. "What you must understand, Mike, is that flea markets are a whole other world, with a hierarchy of their own. If you're selling junk, nobody even knows your name. If you can consistently come up with good pieces, everybody knows who you are. You're the elite, and you'll be courted and you'll be bribed."

"By whom?" Mike asked, obviously intrigued.

"By the compulsive collectors, for one. All the elitists have their list of who collects what. Name and phone number. They pick up a piece, they call. They're wooed by antique dealers, who'll cry or run or pay for first refusal, whatever it takes. Hell, we do it ourselves, Rafe and I. We're not proud. If a vendor has the good stuff, we'll grovel to get to it first. And don't think those buggers don't know it."

"Seems like a crappy way to get stuff," Mike said.

"You mean groveling?" Charlie said. "Hell, groveling's nothing. We know dealers who go to every open house in good neighborhoods and try to bully the owners into selling them the furnishings. Some hardcase dealers follow the obits and hit on the family before the body's cold. One woman we know belongs to four churches so she can skim the cream off the bazaars before the public gets a sniff."

Mike squinted at Charlie. "You do any of that?"

"No," Charlie said. "With us it's business. We're not compulsive. These people are. They've got to have it all. And I mean *all*. Ask Rafe."

Rafe nodded. "Muriel Waller," he said.

"Ah. Muriel Waller." Charlie grinned. "Now, there was one sick puppy."

Mike looked expectantly from Charlie to Rafe and back. "Who was Muriel Waller?" he asked.

Charlie turned to me. "You remember Muriel Waller, don't you, Cat?"

"I remember her. She never washed her hair, she never cut her nails, and she wore the same cotton housedress, winter and summer. She sold the usual Beacon market stuff, but she always had one table of absolutely stunning pieces."

"Yep. And at absolutely stunning prices," Charlie said. "Did you ever go to her house?"

"No. Why?"

"Muriel called us one day, back in our early

years, and told us she wanted to get rid of some stock from her house. So we rushed to her place with our tongues hanging out and every dime we could scrape together.'' Charlie grinned at Rafe. ''Remember?''

Rafe nodded. ''You had to see the place to believe it, Cat. Every room was packed. You walked down alleys between boxes stacked to the ceilings. Every surface was loaded. And none of it was junk. Incredible.''

''Incredible barely describes it,'' Charlie said. ''Whatever we wanted to buy, she wasn't quite ready to part with, not that day. Maybe later. We walked out after two hours, empty-handed, wondering what the hell had just happened.''

''Why wouldn't she sell to you?'' I asked.

''Wait,'' Charlie said, grinning. ''One day, just in passing, we happened to mention the whole weird deal to old Max, and he damn near split a gut laughing. It seems every dealer, every picker, every collector and every vendor in town had the tour at least once. Muriel wasn't selling. She was exhibiting.''

''I don't get it,'' Mike said.

''It was a power trip,'' Charlie told him. ''She had what we wanted, and she made sure we knew it. So we all made nice with Muriel, even when we knew she wasn't going to sell it to us. Like the man said, hope springs eternal.''

''Sick,'' I said.

''It wasn't entirely a power trip with Muriel,''

Rafe added thoughtfully. "She had boxes piled on boxes she hadn't looked into in years, and she was still buying more, often just to make sure nobody else got it. She had to have it all, and she put outrageous prices on things because she couldn't bear to part with them. You're right, Cat, it is a sickness, a disease. I've seen others infected, but none as seriously as Muriel."

"What happened to her?" I asked. "I didn't see her at Finney's or at Beacon."

"She died a couple of years ago. Cancer. And I'm telling you the truth, Cat, she wasn't dead ten minutes before her kids were getting fifty phone calls a day, dealers hotfooting it after all that good stuff of hers."

"What did they do with it all?"

"They had an estate sale," Rafe said.

"The estate sale to end all estate sales." Charlie's grin was wicked. "Everybody and his dog turned out. They were lined up around the block at seven-thirty in the morning, waiting for the door to open at nine. Those kids of Muriel's didn't stand a chance. They had planned to admit ten buyers at a time—some hope. Five seconds after the door opened, the place was bedlam."

"You could barely move," Rafe said. "People weren't being selective, they were grabbing whatever they could reach, rooting through boxes, dropping whatever didn't interest them on the floor. Things were broken, stuff was stolen. We didn't

stay—it was too damn savage—but we were told a
fistfight broke out and a couple of tables went over.
The kids called the police an hour after they opened.
The cops cleared the house and locked the doors,
and that was the end of Muriel's estate sale.''

I had to ask. ''What did the kids end up doing
with her stock? There must have been plenty left.''

''The little bastards gave it all to the Salvation
Army.''

That did it. Charlie, Rafe and I collapsed into rueful laughter.

Mike eyed us suspiciously.

''What's so funny?'' he demanded. ''What's so
damn funny about the Salvation Army?''

''It isn't about the Salvation Army,'' I said, my
laughter dying away. ''And I guess it isn't really
funny. Actually, it's pretty depressing.''

''What is?'' Mike demanded irritably. ''What are
we talking about here?''

''Things,'' I said. ''We're talking about people
acquiring inanimate objects as some kind of creative
expression, as though having a collection gives them
an identity they suspect they might not have otherwise. Nine times out of ten, their kids don't appreciate it or don't want it and all the things they
thought were so rare and precious end up at the Salvation Army. Or in a garage sale. Or a flea market.''

''Where somebody buys it and the cycle starts all
over again,'' Charlie finished cheerfully. ''Flea market vendors make money, antique dealers make

money, and life goes on. What's so depressing about that?''

I shrugged. ''I never thought of it that way. Maybe it is funny at that.''

''You never had the urge to collect anything, Cat?'' Rafe asked.

''Sure,'' I said. ''Money.''

Charlie grinned. ''I'll drink to that,'' he said, and reached for the bottle of ouzo.

''There's only one problem,'' I added, raising my glass to be filled. ''I was never really able get the hang of it.''

Charlie raised his own glass and winked his one golden eye.

''Join the club,'' he said.

# WILLIAM RELLING JR.

## SWEET POISON

### A JACK DONNE MYSTERY

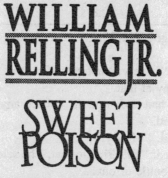

Augustus Poole, the single most influential food and wine critic in the country, is also the most intensely loathed. He insists someone wants him dead. Still, he's been selected to receive a special award at an elite epicurean banquet.

Ex-ATF agent turned vintner Jack Donne has been persuaded to be Poole's bodyguard. As a job, it's murder. Unfortunately the dead man isn't Poole, but rather the banquet's chef, who drank the rare bottle of wine that had been a gift to Poole.

Donne soon finds himself uncorking a mystery as full-bodied as a fine burgundy—aged to murderous perfection by greed, desperation, jealousy…and sour grapes.

*Available January 2000 at your favorite retail outlet.*

# Take 2 books and a surprise gift FREE!

---

## SPECIAL LIMITED-TIME OFFER

---

**Mail to: The Mystery Library™**
**3010 Walden Ave.**
**P.O. Box 1867**
**Buffalo, N.Y. 14240-1867**

**YES!** Please send me **2 free books** from the Mystery Library™ and my free surprise gift. Then send me 3 mystery books, first time in paperback, every month. Bill me only $4.19 per book plus 25¢ delivery and applicable sales tax, if any*. There is no minimum number of books I must purchase. I can always return a shipment at your expense and cancel my subscription. Even if I never buy another book from the Mystery Library™, **the 2 free books and surprise gift are mine to keep forever.**

415 WEN CJQN

---

Name                              (PLEASE PRINT)

---

Address                                                    Apt. No.

---

City                              State                         Zip

---

* Terms and prices subject to change without notice. N.Y. residents add
  applicable sales tax. This offer is limited to one order per household and not
  valid to present subscribers.
© 1990 Worldwide Library.

MYS98

# Denise Dietz

**AN ELLIE BERNSTEIN/
LIEUTENANT
PETER MILLER
MYSTERY**

# Throw Darts at a Cheesecake

# Fat Free Murder

At the weekly meeting of Weight Winners, losing
is everything. Group leader Ellie Bernstein herself
has shed fifty-five pounds, along with a cheating
husband and an unfulfilling life. But she quickly
discovers losing weight is not only murder,
it's downright lethal.

One by one, the group's Big Losers are being
murdered. Is some jealous member of the Friday
meeting a secret killer? Motive aside, Ellie's got
to watch her back as well as her calories before
she finds herself on the most permanent
diet of all...death.

**Available December 1999 at your favorite retail outlet.**

# DEATH OF AN EVANGELISTA

# ALLANA MARTIN

## A TEXANA JONES MYSTERY

When trading post owner Texana Jones discovers
the body of a man in a Mexican taxi, she barely
escapes becoming a scapegoat for corrupt *federales*.
Unfortunately, the innocent cab driver is left
to take the fall.

Then another body is found, leading Texana deeper
into the kinds of secrets that life in the desert hides
well—and the dark places of the human heart
where the borderline between good and evil is
easy to cross....

*Available January 2000 at your favorite retail outlet.*

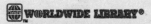 **WORLDWIDE LIBRARY®**

Visit us at www.worldwidemystery.com          WAM335